Bangles and Broken Hearts 3: Return of the Bangles

TAMIA GORE-FELTON

ISBN: 978-1-4834-4829-9 (sc)
ISBN: 978-1-4834-4830-5 (e)

Lulu Publishing Services rev. date: 03/14/2016

Acknowledgements

First and foremost, I would like to thank God for blessing me to be such a creative being. Next, I would like to thank my parents, Patricia Gore and David Rush. Thank you for always being there for me and guiding me in the right direction with your kind and positive words. To my husband Kimo, thank you for being supportive of my dreams and aspirations. To my daughter Kimora, always remember that anything is possible with a lot of determination and dedication. To my beautiful sisters, Angela Gore-Felton and Porscha Rush; I love you two ladies to the moon and back. Thanks for being my assistants, promoters, photographers, proofreaders, and overall handy sidekicks. I would also like to give special thanks to Brandice Gore, Carolyn Bellamy, Allison Hampton, Marvin Latimore, Blac Chyna, Shauntel (Miss. Jackson) Jackson, Marquita (Temper) Brooks, and Kapelieli (Junior) Pome'e.

Dedication

This final tale of sticky situations is dedicated to my loyal readers and supporters. If you purchased a Bangles and Broken Hearts t-shirt, left a review, shared one of my book-related posts, cried when Melody died, or read your copies of Bangles and Broken Hearts over and over again until the next Bangles book was released - put your name on the line below.

(Insert your name here) _____

1

Honeymooning

The day after the wedding I woke up in beautiful Hawaii. While the sun crept over the horizon, Trent snored lightly. I lay naked and listened to the waves crash onto the rocks outside of our villa. After I sat up, I slid on a robe provided by the resort and walked towards the open sliding glass door. I took a deep breath as I stepped onto the balcony. The air smelled like fresh cut pineapples, and the view was out of this world.

As I looked up and down the shore of the beach, I noticed several couples walking hand in hand. I also saw someone writing something in the sand with a stick, a few people jogging, and one shirtless man wore a fanny pack and a pair of white speedos. While he waved a metal detector back and forth over an area of sand, I wondered if he'd ever found anything worthwhile. After watching the man with the metal detector for a few more minutes, I focused my attention back to the beautiful sunrise.

While I leaned over the rail of the balcony, I smiled as I thought to myself. I couldn't believe that I was married. I officially belonged to someone and had a man that belonged to me and only me. I rested my elbows on the railing and bubbled with excitement on the inside until my bare wrist caught my eye. I then thought about my bangles that were locked away inside of mom's safe. It had only been a few weeks since I'd been without my sparkling bracelets and I was still adjusting. I missed them, but the rock on my ring finger made up for all of my missing bling.

Trent did an excellent job picking this ring out. I secretly wondered if someone helped him as I adored the beautiful diamonds. Maybe his mom or even his aunts had suggested rings to him. I don't know, but whoever helped him pick out such a stunning ring deserved a high five because it was perfect. My ring glistened in the sunlight as I moved my hand back and forth and admired the precious stones. I wondered how much it cost as I sat in the wicker chair on the balcony. After I sat back in the chair, I slid off the ring and read the engraved lettering on the inside, "Forever My Love."

When I slipped my ring back on, Trent rolled over in the bed and something caught my eye. Even though he was covered with a thin blanket, his massive erection was very noticeable. I grew hungrier for him by the second as I watched him sleep from the balcony. When the idea of waking him up with a blowjob came to my mind, my bladder interrupted my nasty thoughts and informed me that I had to urinate.

Before I went to the bathroom, I unhooked my cell phone from the charger and powered it on. Since the phone was on silent, it didn't make any annoying beeps or vibrations. After I quietly closed the bathroom door, I turned on the shower. I then sat on the toilet and released the contents of my bladder. When I was done, I continued to sit on the toilet and read through my text messages. All of the messages were congratulatory ones. I smiled as I responded to all the messages with a simple "Thank you."

Just as I was about to get up, I noticed that I had a voicemail message. After I pressed the number one, I heard the voicemail greeting and punched in the five digit code to check my messages. "You have one new voicemail message, to listen press one," said the automated system. I pressed one and listened. My heart dropped when I heard Mont's voice.

"This is the last time I'm going to call you, so you don't have to worry about changing your number. I just wanted you to know that I couldn't sleep, and I was up thinking about you. You're supposed to be my wife, and you know that. You were supposed to be making love to me tonight. I don't think I'll ever get over this, Lyric. I know I said that I would stay away from you but I can't. You're the first thing on my mind when I wake up and the last person I think about before I go to sleep every night. It doesn't matter who I lay beside; I won't be satisfied until it's you. I still love you and want you even though you belong to someone else. I hope Trent treats you right, if he doesn't, just know that I will always be here waiting for you to return to my arms. I love you."

My thoughts swirled as I listened to the message for the second time. I started to delete it, but I wanted Latria to hear this. So I saved the message and powered my phone off. After I flushed the toilet and put my phone on the counter, I stepped into the shower and replayed the message over and over in my head. What was it with Mont? Why couldn't he get over me? Who was I kidding, I knew that I wasn't 100% over him, but I also knew that I wasn't going to return his call. I knew that would lead to something sticky, and I couldn't risk losing Trent again. It just wasn't worth it.

When the bathroom was thick with steam and the smell of fruity body wash filled the air, I dried off. After I dropped the towel to the floor, I brushed my teeth, and grabbed my cell phone from the counter. I then walked back into the bedroom where my husband was still sleeping. After I set my phone on the nightstand, I climbed into bed. Trent still had an erection, but he wouldn't have it much longer because I was about to take care of that. I softly pulled the covers back and climbed on top of him. His warm arms flew around my waist as I whispered, "Good morning handsome."

"Good Morning, Mrs. Morrison," he said, as a smile spread across his face.

"I see that you have a little something going on down there, I hope you don't mind if I take a look," I replied.

"Oh, no, I don't mind at all."

I shimmied down under the covers until I was face to face with his erection. I began to squeeze him seductively with my left hand, and he let out a moan as I took him into my warm mouth. As his erection slid across my lips, I licked, sucked, and stroked him until he climaxed. When I came back up for air, he said, "Damn, am I going to get this every morning or is this just something you're doing for the honeymoon?"

"You could have gotten this on the plane, but that busybody flight attendant wouldn't sit down," I answered, as I wiped my mouth with the back of my hand.

"Um um um," he said, as he kissed me on the cheek before he got out of the bed. "You've got me weak already. How am I supposed to get up and get ready for our day if my knees are weak?"

"I don't know; you'll recover," I chuckled. "Now go shower. I already showered, and I'm ready to eat."

"Yes ma'am," he replied, as he slowly walked to the bathroom.

As he shut the bathroom door, I rolled off the bed, picked my luggage up, and sat it on the bed. After I unzipped the zipper on the first suitcase, I saw that I'd picked up Trent's by mistake and left it open for him. I then opened the next suitcase to find all of my items. The first article of clothing that caught my eye were a pair of cut-off jean shorts. They had so many rips and tears in them that it looked as though Edward Scissorhands designed these shorts himself. I decided that I'd wear the jean shorts and let it all hang out while we were here in Hawaii. I hoped that Trent didn't mind, he'd never seen these shorts before.

I quickly slid the shorts on and chose a yellow halter top and a straw hat to complete my outfit. After I rubbed lotion on my legs, I stepped into a pair of tan leather wedges. I looked good, and I felt great, but Mont's message was beginning to play in my head again. While his voice echoed in my thoughts, I sat on the balcony and tried to clear my mind as Trent finished up in the bathroom.

Before we left our villa, he complimented my outfit and gave me a kiss. I was happy that he didn't say anything about my shorts because I didn't want to change. As the two of us walked hand in hand towards the dining hall, all of the men stopped whatever they were doing when they saw me coming. One man who was sitting with a lady, turned all the way around and watched as I passed by them. The woman looked like she wanted to smack him on the back of the head but she didn't. She only rolled her eyes.

Trent got a kick out of all the men lusting after me. When we were almost to the dining area, he let go of my hand and put his arm around my waist. I could see the envy in the men and women's faces as we strolled by. While the women envied my delicate six pack and the boldness of my outfit, the men envied Trent for being my man. I could tell that a lot of them wanted to be in his shoes. The looks on their faces and the drool that formed in the corners of their mouths gave it away.

When we reached the resort dining hall, the hostess sat us near the bar. I couldn't believe that people were drinking this early in the morning. Other than having an open bar, the resort had a full buffet of breakfast items too. French toast, grits, pancakes, waffles, bacon, ham, sausage, eggs, fresh fruit, cereal, and yogurt. Considering that it was still early in the morning and it was so hot, I only ate fresh fruit and drank a glass of ice water. I didn't want to walk around with a belly full of hot grits in the sweltering heat. That was a recipe for disaster.

While we ate, we discussed the wedding. The first thing Trent mentioned was the gift table.

"Did you see all of those gifts? I wonder what was in all of those boxes."

"Yeah, I hope we got everything that was on our gift registry," I replied.

We had a table full of gifts that we didn't have a chance to look at because we left the reception hall as soon as *Kiss of Life* by Sade played one final time. We had to, if we didn't haul ass, we would've missed our flight. After we both had undressed out of our wedding attire, we threw on some comfy clothes and gathered our luggage from the hatch of my mother's Land Rover. Then we put all of our luggage in the trunk of the limousine, kissed our families goodbye, and departed the venue.

Our loved ones blew bubbles and waved goodbye as the limo pulled out the parking lot. I turned all the way around in the seat and watched them from the back glass until their figures disappeared. While we briskly made our way to the airport, we drank several mini bottles from the bar in the limo. Before Trent started to kiss me, I briefly thought of our families getting to know one another better as they cleaned up the reception hall and talked about how beautiful the wedding was.

Trent interrupted my thoughts of our wedding day when he said, "I can't wait to see the video of the wedding."

"I want to see it too, but we've got three more nights in paradise until then," I replied.

"You looked so damn good in that dress; I wanted to rip it off of you. I couldn't wait until we got here last night," he confessed, with a mischievous smile.

"Well, I'm all yours now," I admitted, as I held up my left hand and flashed my ring at him.

When we were done eating, we started our day. The first thing on our agenda was a boat tour. After a short ride on a golf cart to a tiny pier, we boarded a medium sized boat and I instantly thought of the show *Gilligan's Island*. While I headed for the last two seats under an awning, I remembered the day that Dana taught me how to swim. She was all over me and I didn't even realize it. That girl was a mess, but thanks to her and the huge pool in her parent's backyard, I knew I would survive if the boat capsized. I smiled to myself while the warm breeze swept the thoughts of Dana's wandering hands from my mind. As the boat started to drift from the pier, I checked the buckles on my life jacket and leaned against Trent's shoulder. Not even ten minutes into the tour my eyes dropped to a close and someone yelled, "Look at those dolphins." I jerked my head towards the voice and saw real live dolphins jumping out of the water beside the boat. I immediately thought of Tia and pulled my cell phone out of my purse to see if I could get this action on video.

"Tia's going to love this," I shrilled, as I recorded the dolphins.

"Yes, she is," Trent replied while kissing me on the nape of my neck.

From that point, I wasn't sleepy anymore. I abandoned my cozy seat under the shelter to stand near the railing of the boat. I couldn't wait to see if anything else was going to jump out of the water.

About two hours later, the boat ride was over and my stomach was growling. The fruit I had eaten for breakfast was long gone. As we got into a taxi, Trent asked the driver to take us to the best eatery within a 20-mile radius. The driver nodded his head and drove about ten or twelve miles before we came to a stop.

"All three of these restaurants have incredibly delicious food. You'll have to decide which one you want to give a try," said the driver.

"Okay, thank you," replied Trent, as he handed the man a few bills for our ride.

After Trent and I got out of the cab, we were left with the decision of deciding on a restaurant. All three of the restaurants were painted in bright colors. One was red, another was yellow, and the other was orange. The orange restaurant had a line out the door and down the sidewalk. I knew that had to be a good thing, but the way my stomach was growling, I couldn't wait that much longer.

The red restaurant had a blinking sign that flashed, "Best Loco Moco in Town." I didn't know what Loco Moco was, but it reminded me of the old song *The Locomotion.* That's why I chose the red restaurant. As we walked past the yellow restaurant, a sweet smell nearly made me change my mind, but we continued toward the flashing sign. When we walked through the door, a pleasant aroma of grilled pork flew up my nostrils. My stomach growled even louder, and I looked up at Trent to see if he heard the ferocious grumble, but he didn't.

Walking inside of the eatery gave my body a feeling of coolness. I wanted to thank the management for having the thermostat set on such a cool setting. As the sweat dried from my shoulders and brow, I looked around and saw how quaint the place was. The brick walls were plastered with pictures of sunsets and oceans. The place was pretty crowded, and there was a small line of folks at the hostess station.

While we waited, I looked around at everything and everybody until it was our turn to be seated. When we were next in line at the hostess station, the lady flashed us a toothy grin and said, "Thank you for choosing our restaurant. Please follow me to your table." The petite hostess walked us quickly through a maze of occupied tables and stopped at a table near the flashing Loco Moco sign. As soon as we sat down, she handed us our menus and pointed to the specials written on a chalkboard. I hadn't paid any attention to that sign when I was in the line.

Trent and I both thumbed through the menus. It took me a minute to make my mind up, but he blurted out what he wanted to order.

"I'm going to have the BBQ pork sandwich with the grilled pineapples."

"Alright, I'm not sure what I want just yet," I responded.

"Take your time baby, I'm going to go to the restroom. If the waitress comes while I'm gone, order my food for me please," he said, as he got up and walked away from the table.

"Sure thing," I answered.

While I continued to study the menu, I heard a baritone voice say, "What can I get you to drink?" When I looked up, I wanted to scream. This had to be the finest man I had ever laid eyes on. He stood about 6 feet tall, had long wavy hair, tan skin, dimples, and a beautiful smile. He was dressed in all black, and his name tag read, "Jason." After I had zoomed in on his face, I saw that he had blue-gray eyes just like my dad.

"I'll have a glass of ice water and a strawberry daiquiri," I requested.

"No, problem, may I see your ID?" He asked as I looked at him with lustful eyes.

"You sure can," I said, as I dug into my small purse.

When I retrieved my driver's license, he studied it for a brief second and handed it back to me.

"I have some family that lives in Virginia, I was there last month," he announced, while he looked at my cleavage.

"Oh, really?" I responded inquisitively, with a sneaky smile.

"Yep, I'll have your drink out in just a bit."

As he started to walk away, I yelled, "Excuse me, may I also have a sweet tea for my husband?"

"Yes ma'am, I'll add it to your order," Jason said.

I took a deep breath after I ordered Trent's drink. I didn't know what was taking Trent so long in the bathroom, but I wanted him to come back soon. I feared that the old Lyric was about to surface and ask Jason for his phone number. If Trent didn't come back first, I was going to ask Jason for his number. I had to; I just couldn't pass up all of that masculinity. When I saw Jason heading back to the table with our beverages, I thought of how I would ask for his number. I didn't see anything wrong with having a plan B, just in case my marriage didn't work out.

As soon as he set the drinks down in front of me, I opened my mouth to ask for his number, and Trent sat down. I quickly changed,

"So how can I reach you Jason" into "Thank you" as I looked up into his beautiful eyes.

"You're welcome. Are you ready to place your order now?" He asked as I took a sip of my water.

"Yes, we are," Trent blurted out.

After he ordered quickly, I ordered the first thing I saw on the chalkboard that was directly behind Jason.

"I'll try the Loco Moco," I said with a smile.

"You won't be disappointed. We have the best Loco Moco in town," he confirmed, as he wrote down our orders.

By the time our food came out, I'd already drank my strawberry daiquiri and ordered another. I didn't really want another one; I only wanted to see Jason again. This time, he handed my drink to me instead of putting it down on the table. Our hands touched for a brief second, and he smiled, showing his dangerously deep dimples.

Meanwhile, Trent was gulping down his sweet tea. When Jason brought our food to the table, my mouth watered as steam rose from the plates. The smell of onions, peppers, beef, and pork made me forget about the table manners that my mother had taught me. I was slurping and smacking on all the delicious food. I even wiped my mouth with the back of my hand. When I saw Jason walking over with a picture of sweet tea, I got my act together real quick.

While he poured Trent more sweet tea, he stared at me and almost overflowed his cup. Trent didn't even notice because he was focused on his ketchup covered french fries. Before I could stop myself, I winked one of my eyes at Jason, and he licked his lips as he placed the check face down on the table. I could feel my panties growing moist, and I knew that this was wrong on so many levels. I hadn't even been married for 48 hours, and I was already acting like a whore.

I had to do better. I couldn't start my marriage off like this. For goodness sake, I had just got Trent back, and I didn't want to mess up.

So I took one long last lustful look at Jason and didn't look his way again the entire time we were at the little red restaurant.

"What's the damage?" Trent asked as he turned over the check. "Wow, only $50 bucks. That wasn't bad at all. Did you want to order something to go, baby?"

Even though the Loco Moco was delicious, I wanted to order Jason to go, but I knew that I couldn't do that. So I replied, "Nope. I'm good."

After Trent pulled out his wallet, he retrieved three twenty dollar bills and lay them on top of the check. He then took a final gulp of his sweet tea and asked if I was ready to go. With a nod of my head, we both stood up and left the red restaurant. While we walked down the sidewalk, I couldn't help but notice that the orange restaurant still had a long line. I tried to peek into the window of the restaurant, but I couldn't see much of anything.

While Trent hailed a cab, I looked back at the orange restaurant and wondered if they had waiters that looked like Jason working inside of them too. "Let's go," he said, as he reached out for my hand. We stood on a curve, and a cab stopped right in front of us. Before Trent opened the door of the cab, he said, "I'm sorry. Did you want to walk around a little more or would you like to go back to the villa?"

"Let's go back to the villa. Maybe we can get a quick nap. Then I think we should lay on the beach and watch the sunset later," I said.

"That sounds good to me," he replied, as we both slid into the cab and buckled our seat belts.

The ride back to the resort was a little bumpy, and it felt like I was being rocked to sleep. I couldn't wait to get out of that cab and into the soft bed in our villa. When the car approached the resort, Trent pulled out his wallet again, but I told him to put it up. I then reached into my purse and paid the driver for our ride.

"Now that's what I'm talking about," he said. I laughed as I slid across the vinyl seat once more. After Trent shut the door to the cab, we walked hand in hand into the resort.

2

Home Sweet Home

After a few more days of fun and sun, our honeymoon was over, and we were waving goodbye to Hawaii. When we boarded the plane, butterflies formed in the pit of my stomach because we were going to be in the air for a long time. I'd flown before when I was with Know Betta and his crew, but we didn't fly over so much water. I was cool with it on the way to Hawaii because it was dark and I couldn't see the water below. With our plane leaving bright and early this morning, I knew I was going to see everything when we took off.

Trent and I were lucky enough to sit in a row by ourselves. After we buckled up, we listened to all the passenger announcements. The flight attendants then had a seat, and the plane started to move. I took a deep breath and tried not to look out of the window as the plane took off and ascended. I felt lightheaded as I shut my eyes tight and prayed until I heard one of the flight attendants ask, "Ma'am, would you care for a beverage?"

"Yes, a bottle of water will be fine," I responded as I looked over at Trent.

I nudged him to see if he wanted a drink, but he was already sleeping. I swear that man could fall asleep fast. When the flight attendant handed me my water, I paid her and told her thank you. She then continued her way down the aisle with her rolling cart full of beverages. With nothing else to do, I took my phone out of my purse and connected my headphones. After watching the video I'd taken of the dolphins, it made me anxious to see Tia. I couldn't wait to show her the video and see her little face light up.

After going through all the pictures and videos that were on my phone, I tried to go to sleep. As I leaned my head back against my travel pillow, the thought of Mont's voicemail came to mind. From that thought, I knew that I wasn't going to be able to fall asleep. Knowing that I was going home meant that I may encounter Mont sooner or later. My nerves were an absolute mess, and I looked out of the window at the puffs of clouds.

The next thing I knew, Trent was tapping me on the shoulder, telling me to wake up. The plane had landed, and the passengers were already getting off. I couldn't believe that I'd fallen asleep and slept through the landing. Without saying anything, I gave Trent a smile and unbuckled my seat belt. After I stood up, he waited and let me get in line in front of him. While we waited for someone's grandmother to get out of her seat. Trent rubbed his private up against my behind. I turned and looked at him and said, "When we get in the limo, it's on."

The grin on Trent's face was wide. I giggled to myself as I realized how much this man meant to me. As we walked through the airport, he held my hand and even kissed the back of it while we waited for our luggage at the baggage return. When I spotted our luggage, I pointed to our brown leather suitcases. After we made sure that we had all of our bags in tow, we headed towards the lobby of the airport.

The limousine driver was waiting for us at the entry of the airport. He wore all black and held a white sign that read Mr. & Mrs. Trenton

Morrison. I smiled as we approached the thin man. "I'll get your bags," he said after he opened the limo door for us. We climbed inside, and the driver shut the door behind us.

While the driver loaded our luggage into the trunk, we watched him out the back window. You couldn't be too careful these days. He could have sold our luggage to someone in the parking lot. When the driver closed the trunk, we both turned around and looked at each other.

"Didn't you promise me something on the plane?" Trent asked.

"You are so nasty," I whispered as I mounted his lap and kissed him.

His hands wandered under my t-shirt and unfastened my bra with no problem. I slowly rocked back and forth on top of him, as I bent down so my head wouldn't hit the ceiling of the car. We kissed and fondled each other until we couldn't take it anymore, then we pulled our shorts off, and he bent me over the seat. Shortly after he entered me, I dissolved right in front of him. He continued to deliver deep rhythms of thrusts as I held in my moans. I wanted to yell out, but I didn't want the driver to hear me, so I buried my face in the seat. I was lost somewhere in a trance as I climaxed and Trent's pace quickened. As he withdrew himself from my slippery opening, a bit of his love juices spilled onto the carpet of the limo.

When we'd caught our breath, we pulled up our shorts and quickly fixed ourselves up. After I fastened the clasps on my bra, I helped myself to a bottle of juice in the mini fridge. I drank the whole bottle down so fast that Trent didn't have time to ask for any. I wondered where we were as I rolled the black tinted window down. We were so busy getting it on; we didn't even notice how close we were to being home. In less than five minutes we would be reunited with our home and all the gifts from the wedding.

After doing all of that huffing, puffing, and sweating on the leather in the back of the limo. I was hot and wanted to take a refreshing shower.

"What do you want to do after we get unpacked?" Trent asked.

"Umm, take a shower and pick up Tia. Then we can all lay on the couch and watch television," I replied as the limo started to slow down.

"That sounds like a plan," Trent chimed, as we heard the driver exit the limo and open the trunk.

Instead of waiting for the driver to open the door, I let myself out of the limo. I felt the need to stretch until I saw cars parked in the driveway. There were three familiar Cadillac's, mom's Land Rover, my mother-in-law's Subaru, and a few more vehicles. As I wondered what was going on, the driver looked at me like I was crazy for opening my door.

"What in the world is going on?" I said.

"It looks like a welcome back party," he responded.

"Did you know anything about this?" I asked as I grabbed the handle to a rolling suitcase and one of our small carry-on bags. I struggled with the bag because we'd bought back way more stuff than we took. We did a little shopping at the mall and got souvenirs for everyone. Some people were going to receive t-shirts, others would only receive key chains, or shot glasses. As I looked at the cars in the driveway, I hoped that we had enough gifts for everyone inside.

"Nope, I had no clue," he replied before we stepped onto the porch.

"It smells like someone made peach cobbler," I said, as my nostrils flared and mouth watered.

Trent tried the knob, but the door was locked, so he reached into his pocket for his keys. Just as he pulled his set of keys out, the entry door flew open, and voices yelled, "Welcome back."

While everyone celebrated, Tia jumped into Trent's arms and gave him a great big hug. Next, it was my turn, hugging her small body felt remarkable. I knew that I missed her, but the way my heart felt at this very moment was indescribable. After everyone hugged us, we were swept away to the dining room. There were lots of balloons, a buffet of food, and even a welcome back cake. I was so surprised.

"I hope you guys are hungry," Trent's mother yelled, as she pointed in the direction of the buffet.

"If I wasn't I'd make room for it," I replied.

Shortly after we greeted everyone, we all washed our hands and my mother said the grace. Then we all sat down at the crowded table and began to talk. My plate was piled high with fried chicken, rice, gravy, butter beans, candy yams, and cabbage. While everyone asked questions about Hawaii, Trent and I talked with our mouths full. We were just as excited about being back home and had forgotten our manners. "Oh, Tia we saw dolphins. I have a video on my phone," I said, as I dropped my fork and reached inside of my purse.

When I pulled out my phone, everyone crowded around as Tia sat excitedly on my lap. Everyone loved the footage of the dolphins. After they watched the clip of the video a few more times, I suggested that Trent pull out his phone to show the family the rest of the pictures. He hesitated at first, but everyone started crowding around him, so he opened his phone. Right away, I noticed the text message indicator on the top of the screen. As he flipped through the images, he told everybody what the pictures were. While a few family members asked questions about the beautiful images, my eyes watched the little white envelope at the top of the screen. That's when another message flashed across the top that notified him of a picture message.

As soon as the message flashed across the top of the screen, Trent dropped his phone and pretended that it wouldn't come back on. Everyone else believed his lie. But I saw him power the phone off when he picked it up off of the floor. As everyone remained huddled around him, he began to panic and pretended to press the power button on the side of the phone. "Well, I guess we'll see the pictures later. If my phone decides to come back on," he said, as he pushed it deep inside of his pants pocket.

I started to make a big fuss, but I didn't want the family to see us fighting. This was a welcome home party, so I grabbed a few bottles of wine and started drinking. To my surprise, Trent's aunts drank a glass of wine with me. While we talked and ate, Trent kept getting up and going into the kitchen or to the bathroom. I didn't know what he was doing, but he was making me suspicious.

After the kitchen was clean, Trent and I distributed the souvenirs. We had just enough gifts for everybody, and I was glad because I didn't want anyone to feel left out. When my mother left, I got Tia ready for a bath. While she was in the tub, she splashed and played with the bubbles. The bubbles reminded me of the clouds that we passed by in the sky today on the airplane.

When Tia was all done with her bath, I read her a story and listened as she said her prayers. After she was tucked in and three of her favorite teddy bears were in bed with her, I gave her a kiss on the forehead. Before I left her room, I turned off the light and clicked on the nightlight. With her room door ajar, I made my way to my bedroom.

I heard Trent talking to one of his uncles, as I shut our bedroom door. I immediately undressed and started the shower as soon as I walked into our spacious bathroom. As the steam began to rise, I weighed myself. 132 pounds, I still weighed the same as last week. I thought eating all of that delicious food in Hawaii would have put a few pounds on me, but I was wrong. Regardless of if I'd gained any weight or not, I knew that I had to get back in the gym with Latria.

In the shower, I washed my hair and thought of calling Latria to tell her about Mont's message and the dreamy waiter at the restaurant in Hawaii. I wish I'd taken a picture with him so she could see how handsome he was. Describing him in words simply wasn't good enough. While I was lost in my thoughts, I didn't even hear the bedroom door open.

When Trent said, "Well, everyone is gone," it startled me, and I almost slipped in the tile shower.

"You scared me. I almost fell," I shouted, as I rinsed the remainder of the suds from my hair and body.

"I'm sorry baby, you know I wouldn't want anything to happen to you. I'm going to get one of those non-slip mats for the shower floor tomorrow."

"I know it, it's okay," I said, as I turned the shower off and stepped out.

Trent started to run a bath, while I wrapped a towel around myself and towel dried my hair. We talked about the party and Hawaii, while I started my nighttime beauty regimen. I soaked cotton balls in astringent and dabbed my face with them. Next, I tweezed my eyebrows, brushed and flossed my teeth, and applied an expensive moisturizer on my face. When I was finished, Trent was done taking his bath and in bed.

After I slipped on a thin nightshirt that I'd gotten as a gift from our wedding shower, I lay down beside him and turned the television. He'd been watching a deep sea fishing show before he fell asleep. As I flipped through the channels, I ran across *The Cosby Show*. In this particular episode, Theo got his ear pierced without permission. I laughed quietly, as I watched two more episodes before I turned the television off.

I tried counting sheep and drank a cup of hot tea, but I couldn't sleep. I wished that I'd never noticed the message on Trent's phone earlier. I wondered what or who the picture was of that he'd received. While he lay there snoring with a stomach full of soul food and wine, I snatched the covers off of him. He didn't even wake up. That's when the thought of going through Trent's phone entered my mind. After trying to talk myself out of it, I was already tiptoeing around the bed.

I know- it was terrible, I had very little self-control. As I made my way around our King size bed, I looked for his phone. After going through his pants pocket from earlier and not finding a thing, I noticed the phone was sitting right on top of his nightstand. The blinking blue light caught my eye. I wasn't sure if it meant that he'd missed a call or if he had a new text message.

After I swallowed the spit that was in my mouth, I carefully picked up the phone and headed towards my closet. When I walked in, I quietly closed the door and made my way to the vanity. I clicked on the light, and my face was illuminated in the dark closet. When I sat the phone down on the counter, I thought about how looking at this message could change my feelings towards my husband. I meditated as the blinking light continued to tease me. It drove me crazy, and I immediately picked the phone up and pressed the button towards the bottom of the screen.

The whole thing lit up, and a white envelope was sitting in the upper left corner. My heart beat wildly, as I tapped the envelope with my finger. After my eyes read the name Diamond, they flew to the remainder of the text and read the message. "Did you like the picture that I sent you earlier? Why didn't you respond? You must've been around your wife." My heart pounded as if it were an 808 drum machine and my mouth was so hot that if I tried to spit, steam would've come out.

There was another text that was an image, but it wouldn't download. I wondered what the image could be. As I sat there and watched the phone like a television, but the image never downloaded. In a way, I was glad that I couldn't see what the picture was. I didn't know what I would have done if an image of a naked body would have appeared on the screen.

My emotions were already getting the best of me. I was ready to hurt someone, preferably this Diamond person or Trent. When warm tears dropped out of my eyes and onto my cheeks, I knew that I had to come to grips with what was happening. Before I turned into the Incredible Hulk and started to burst out of my nightshirt, I sat down in the chair in front of my vanity. When I looked in the mirror, I asked myself one question. *"Could I deal with a cheating husband?"*

That's when a voice from within yelled, *"Hell No."* As much as I wanted to listen to the voice, I thought, *"I have a nice life, beautiful house, and a fat bank account. Surely, I can deal with this until I find out more about this Diamond person."* The best thing I could do at the moment is gather more information, before jumping to conclusions.

Although this seemed like a sexual text, it may be something else to this, and I knew that Latria could help me get to the bottom of this. With her on my team, I knew I'd know what in the hell was going on in little or no time. After I dried my eyes into the collar of my nightshirt, I switched off the light on the vanity and made my way to my closet door.

When I opened my closet door, Trent wasn't in bed to my surprise. I heard a steady stream of urine hitting the water in the toilet.

"You alright baby?" He asked.

I jumped and nervously ran to put his phone back on his nightstand.

"Yeah, I'm okay."

"Where were you?" He asked as he got back on the bed.

"I went to check on Tia," I lied, as I slid closer to him. Not even a minute later he was asleep, but I continued to toss and turn until I finally drifted off.

I didn't remember having a dream that night, all I remember was waking up to a burning smell. As soon as I opened my eyes, the smoke detector came on, and I heard Tia screaming. *"What the hell?"* I thought, as I jumped up and ran to the kitchen to see Trent opening the oven, and black smoke flying out.

"Daddy you forgot about the biscuits," Tia yelled, from the living room.

"Aww, shucks!" He grunted as he put the pan of biscuits that resembled lumps of charcoal on top of the stove.

I promptly opened the window over the kitchen sink and opened the screen door in the living room.

"What in the world were you doing Trent? You could've burned the house down?" I yelled, in an irritated voice.

"Daddy was on the phone in the garage," Tia tattled, without even turning her head from watching *SpongeBob*.

"I was attempting to make you breakfast in bed, but I had an important phone call that I had to take," he replied while he started tossing the burnt biscuits in the trash can.

"Oh really," I thought to myself. Without getting an attitude, I suggested that we go out for breakfast. That way we could open up all the windows and the house could air out. After we all got dressed, I put Tia's hair into one big ponytail and we left.

As Trent drove around the loop in our driveway, I sat quietly.

"Do you want Denny's, Shoney's, or IHOP?" He asked as he made a left onto the highway.

"Let Tia choose," I suggested, as I started texting Latria.

"Daddy do they have crabby patties at Denny's?" She asked.

"They might, is that where you want to go?" As they continued to carry on their conversation about crabby patties and what not, I blocked both of them out.

I only heard the little voice inside of my head telling me what to text Latria. My fingers moved quickly over the screen of my iPhone as I filled her in on what happened. I told her how Trent pretended to drop his phone at the welcome back party yesterday, the text message from Diamond, and the smoky house that I woke up to this morning. As she responded to my text messages, I could hear her foul language as if she was sitting right next to me.

By the time we made it to the restaurant, I'd successfully text Latria about the whole Diamond situation. She wanted to text more, but I told her I wasn't able to because we were almost at the restaurant. When Trent pulled into the parking lot at Denny's, I sent her one final text message before deleting our entire conversation. Just as I was about to put my phone in my purse, a text message popped up that read, "We're going to find out who this Diamond bitch is. Try not to worry." With Latria on my side, I knew that we were going to find out what was going on. I wasn't sure if I was ready for the truth though.

3

Birth Control

After Trent had turned off the car we both got out, and I helped Tia out of her car seat. Then we walked into Denny's, and the hostess showed us to our seats. While she told us about the specials, she handed us each a menu. Just as I was about to close my menu, the waitress came with her pen and order pad in hand. "Good morning, can I start you off with some coffee or cocoa today?" She asked.

"Umm, I'll take a glass of orange juice, and I'd like to place my food order if that's ok."

The waitress shook her head, and I kept talking.

"I'll have the Moons over my Hammy with extra cheese, please."

"Sure thing ma'am. Sir, what can I get for you and the little lady?"

"Do you serve crabby patties?" Trent inquired.

Meanwhile, Tia watched her dad and the waitress tentatively. The waitress looked confused and replied, "Like the ones on *SpongeBob*? No sir, but.." and that's all she could say before Tia started whining.

She then had the meltdown of all meltdowns.

"Daddy, I want a crabby patty. You said they had them," she yelled.

I was beyond embarrassed as Tia started to sob louder and louder.

"Let me see if we can make one for her," the waitress said, as she walked away from the table quickly.

When snot shot out of Tia's nose, the people that were sitting behind us got up and moved. I wanted to get away from Tia too. I didn't know what I'd gotten myself into and had to remember to take my birth control pill tonight.

Before the waitress could return I reached for my purse and said, "Let's go." I stormed out of the restaurant and waited outside by the car until Trent, and our cry baby came out. While Tia wiped her snotty nose in her shirt, Trent begged me to come back inside, but I refused. We ended up leaving Denny's and went to the drive through at a nearby Bojangles'.

"Here's your crabby patty," I said, as I handed Tia a golden brown sausage biscuit.

"Thank you Mommy Lyric," she responded.

I then looked at Trent; he didn't look back, but I knew he saw me staring at him out of the corner of his eye. I was thankful that the drive back home was quiet. I had a slight headache and wanted nothing more than to go to Latria's house and lay on her soft plum sofa for a couple of hours. After I had finished off my orange juice, I realized that I could have used a shot of liquor in it. As we pulled up in our driveway, I prayed that the house didn't smell like smoke anymore.

When Trent turned the engine of the car off, his cell phone rang. I didn't move because I wanted to see if he was going to answer the call. After he looked at the phone, he pressed the reject button and looked at me. "Aren't you going to get out of the car?" He asked. As bad as I wanted to ask him why he didn't answer the call, I resisted the urge and said, "Yeah."

I opened my car door and got out, then I opened Tia's door and reached inside to unbuckle her out of her car seat. Just as I picked her up and put her on my hip, Trent's cell phone rang again. I wondered if he was going to answer the call when I shut the car door. He answered the call and I looked back into the car window and he didn't bother to look up. *"Who could he be talking to?"* I thought, as I carried Tia up the sidewalk and onto the porch. I felt my face getting hotter by the second and I wanted to cry, but I didn't want to do it in front of Tia.

After I put her down on the porch, I looked back at Trent. He was smiling and talking on the phone in the car. I wanted to smack that stupid grin off of his face, but instead, I reached into my purse and took out my keys.

"Mommy Lyric, I have to use the bathroom," Tia said, as she started to do a little dance.

"Okay baby, hold it until I unlock the door," I replied, as I turned the doorknob and pushed the door open.

"I can't hold it, Mommy Lyric," she said, as we ran into the house that still smelled like smoke.

When we reached the bathroom, she confirmed that she'd wet her pants. There also was a trail of urine from the front door to the bathroom. I wanted to scream, I couldn't take this aggravation much longer, I had to get the hell out of there.

When Tia started to cry, I felt sorry for her, so I cleaned her up and picked out some dry clothes for her to put on. Just as I was getting the mop out, Trent came into the house.

"Why are you mopping? The floors were clean," he said.

"Tia had an accident. She's all cleaned up now, though," I replied.

"Oh, well I've got to make a run. I'll be back in a few hours. Something came up at the funeral home, and the director insists that I come in."

"Is that who was on the phone?" I asked as I filled the mop bucket with hot soapy water.

"Yeah, an old man passed away. Poor guy, they found him dead inside of his house. They say he was dead for two or three days already, so he has to be embalmed today."

"That's terrible," I agreed. "So when do you think you'll be back? I wanted to go to Latria's for a while."

"Maybe in a couple of hours, that's if nothing else happens," he said.

"Oh okay, I guess I'll go over to Latria's tonight."

When I finished mopping the floor, Trent was long gone. I went to turn the television down in the living room and saw that Tia had fallen asleep. I let out a deep breath and turned the television off before I put all the windows down.

I was glad that Tia was asleep, so I could have a moment to myself. I'd only been married for seven days and I felt wore out already. With the house quiet, I remembered to take my birth control pill. After I had swallowed the tiny pill, I climbed on my bed and called Latria. I knew she was going to be pissed when she found out that I might not be able to come over today. As I plopped down on the bed in my room, I dialed Latria's number and waited for her to answer the phone.

"Are you on your way over?" She blurted, as soon as she answered the phone.

"Girl, no. Trent had to go to the funeral home and prepare a body," I explained.

"Aww shit, I don't want to hear nothing about that creepy mess."

I then let out a little laugh and started to tell her about Tia's meltdown at Denny's.

"That girl needs her behind popped; I bet she would have straightened up then."

"Trent doesn't pop her. He uses time-out, and I don't know how I feel about putting my hands on people's kids," I confessed.

"What do you mean people's kids? Tia is your child too, you and Trent need to talk about that."

"Yeah, you're right, I said in a somber tone. Then I remembered the voicemail from Mont and blurted, "Please tell me that you're sitting down!"

"Oh my God, what happened?" She squealed. "Mont left me a voicemail message the night of the wedding," I whispered.

"No he didn't!" She responded.

"Oh, yes he did too. Hold on, I'm going to connect the voicemail on three-way, so you can hear it," I excitedly said, as I switched the line over and joined the call.

Latria listened quietly while Mont spilled his guts. After listening to the message once, she immediately asked to hear the message again.

"Damn, that's a mess right there. So have you called him?"

"Hell no. If I open up that can of worms, I'd be divorced quicker than Brittney Spears was."

"You are crazy. Are you going to call him?" She asked in a serious tone.

"I doubt it. Things would have to get awfully bad if I ever decided to call him," I confessed.

"I understand. So how was the honeymoon?" Latria chuckled.

"It was absolutely amazing, the villa was the bomb. The view was phenomenal, and we had the best sex. We went on a hike, a boat tour, to a sunset luau, and we ate at some great restaurants."

As soon as I said the word restaurant, I thought about the handsome waiter that I met at the red restaurant.

"That reminds me, I met the most attractive man that I'd ever lay eyes on in Hawaii."

"Hold on, while you were on your honeymoon, you were checking out guys?"

"Yep, I sure was," I cackled.

"Let me fix a drink before you start," she said.

Needless to say, I didn't wait for her to fix a drink. I just blurted out everything that happened at the red restaurant. First I described Jason to Latria. "He had golden skin, dimples, straight teeth, blue-gray eyes, muscles, beautiful wavy hair and two Hawaiian tattoos." Just saying those wonderful keywords in one sentence made Latria take a deep breath. I knew for a fact that I had her undivided attention.

I continued to brag, "I know that he was interested in me. The way he looked at me told me that I was his type."

"So while the two were making googly eyes at one another, where in the hell was Trent?" She asked.

"That reminds me, he went to the bathroom for a long ass time. That's how Jason and I got acquainted and girl, check this out. When I ordered my drink, Jason asked to see my ID. When he saw that I lived in Virginia, he stated that he'd recently been here to visit."

"Damn girl, that is crazy. Do you think he remembered your name or address?"

"I don't know; that's my old address. If he remembers it, he'll end up at my old apartment. I said, as the both of us laughed.

When we were done talking about my Hawaiian crush, we moved on to the sensitive subject, the Diamond woman.

"So what do you think took Trent so long in the bathroom at the restaurant?"

"I'm not sure, he'd eaten a big breakfast that morning. Maybe he was taking a dump," I joked.

"Or maybe he was texting or talking to Diamond in the bathroom," she suggested.

"Maybe he was," I replied, in a dry tone. I don't know what to do, and I'm scared as hell to find out the truth, that's why I doubt if I dig any deeper."

"Lyric, over the years I've grown to love you like the sister I've never had. I'll be damn if I stand by and let Trent make a fool out of you.

There's no need for you to do the digging because I'll do it for you. As soon as I get to the DMV in the morning, I'm going to enter Diamond into the database and see how many women pop up with that scandalous name. Hopefully, the chick has a driver's license and is in the system. All I need you to do is to see if you can check Trent's phone again tonight when he gets home. We need this slut's phone number."

After two hours of planning and plotting with Latria, I cut the conversation short when I heard Tia walk into my bedroom. The way she tattled on Trent this morning, I knew that I had to be careful around her. Tia was probably more dangerous that a mini tape recorder.

"Mommy Lyric, I'm hungry," she said, as she stood at the foot of the bed.

"Okay, baby. Let's see what Mommy Lyric can whip up for you," I said, as we headed to the kitchen. How about some nachos?" I asked while I poured a drink for myself.

The chilled shot of Gray Goose set my throat on fire, but the buzz was well worth it. I felt like I was on a cloud after I drank another shot and sat with Tia at the counter. By the time the sun had set, I knew that I wouldn't be going to visit Latria tonight because Trent wasn't home. As a matter of fact, I hadn't heard anything from him.

That's when the negative thoughts started to run through my head. *"Was he with this Diamond person? If so, what were they doing and where were they doing it?"* Just the thought of someone getting down and dirty with my husband set me on fire. I couldn't imagine someone else teasing him with their tongue or them kissing his soft full lips. I had to do something to take my mind off of him, so I offered to paint Tia's toes.

Tia chose the color pink. Out of all the nail polish that I had, I knew that she was going to pick the bubble gum pink color. I think that pink was every little girl's favorite color. Even though I did an excellent job painting Tia's toes, they ended up looking a hot mess. She wouldn't be still, so I didn't dare make the suggestion to paint her fingernails. Since she already had pink polish on my white comforter; I decided that we'd better move this party into the living room before she messed up anything else.

On our way to the living room, I looked out of the window and saw that Trent's car was parked in the yard. I wondered how long he'd been home when I looked closer; I saw that he was in the car with the phone up to his ear. I couldn't believe this man, he was pushing me close to the edge and he didn't even know it.

After about ten minutes had passed, I heard him enter the foyer. Tia ran to him, and he scooped her up with ease.

"Daddy, where were you? You were gone too long. Mommy Lyric and I ate nachos, and she painted my toes," Tia said, as she pointed down at her feet.

"Mommy Lyric is so sweet; I'm going to paint her toes later," he replied, as he sat down next to me on the couch.

"No thank you," I coldly said, and got up off of the sofa.

No man had ever painted my toes and I wanted Trent too, but I didn't let him. I was disgusted with the fact that he could be so blatant by talking to another woman in our driveway. Not to mention that when he sat down next to me on the couch, he smelled like formaldehyde and perfume. So, there was some truth to his story. Without confirming it with him, I knew that he went to work at the funeral home and that he'd been with a lady.

That wasn't my perfume that was lingering on his clothes. I didn't wear that old lady, church smelling perfume. It was a strong scent, almost like an Elizabeth Arden fragrance from back in the day. When I made it to my bedroom, I closed the door. What I really wanted to do is go to Latria's house, but I knew that I needed to get Trent's phone again. I had to see what number this Diamond woman was calling him from.

I made sure I stayed in my bedroom. I heard Trent as he got Tia ready for bed. Water splashed, songs were sung, and stories were read.

When I heard small footsteps running in the direction of my room, I knew that Tia was coming to say good night. I pretended to watch television as she busted through the room door.

"Good night Mommy Lyric, I love you. Have sweet dreams okay," she said before she jumped on the bed and gave me a big hug and a kiss.

"I love you too," I responded, as she jumped down and ran past Trent.

"I'm going to lay down with her until she falls asleep," he announced before he shut our bedroom door back.

I wonder why he decided to lay with Tia. *"Was he trying to kill time, so I would fall asleep and wouldn't ask him questions? Did he realize that he smelled like perfume?"* My mind was full of questions, and I was tiring myself out thinking about all the possibilities of why Trent stayed in Tia's room for an entire hour.

I fell asleep waiting for him to come to bed. When I woke up, the room smelled like men's body wash, the television was off, and Trent was in the bed next to me. I could have kicked myself when I realized that I'd fallen asleep waiting for him to come back from Tia's room. I looked at the clock to see what time it was, and three hours passed since Tia had kissed me good night.

With thoughts of counting sheep crossed my mind, I saw the blink of a blue light coming from Trent's nightstand. I knew that his phone had a message or missed call and I had to get up and get that phone. I had to see what Diamond's number was so I could give it to Latria. While Trent rested his heavy arm was around my waist; I tried to think of a way to get out of bed without waking him up. While he continued to snore, I came to the conclusion that I was trapped and gave up. Just as I shut my eyes, Trent turned over and I was no longer his prisoner. That meant his face was now facing his nightstand, and that's exactly where the glow of the blinking blue light was coming from.

After debating with myself for a few minutes, I eased off of the bed. Just like last night, I tiptoed to his nightstand and scooped the phone up like a newborn baby. Only this time, I took the phone into the bathroom and not the closet. As I sat the phone down on the counter it started to vibrate. It scared the mess out of me, and I almost screamed. When the screen lit up, there wasn't a name or number, the word **UNKNOWN** flashed across the screen.

As bad as I wanted to answer the call, I didn't. When the phone finally stopped vibrating, I pressed the button near the bottom of the screen only to learn that Trent had put a lock on his phone. A keypad of numbers popped up, and I was completely taken by surprise. I didn't know what his code could have been.

With my heart thumping rapidly inside of my chest. I punched in Tia's birthday, Trent's birthday, and even my birthday. I had no luck, and the phone flashed the message: Incorrect PIN entered. It looked as if I wouldn't get into Trent's phone tonight, I had no clue what the pin could have been. After three wrong attempts, I gave up. I couldn't wait to tell Latria, this made him look real bad. He'd never had a reason to lock his phone before. There had to be something going on.

On the way back into the bedroom, I stubbed my toe on the side of the dresser and almost woke Trent up when I yelled. His body turned over again and curled into a fetal position, as I quickly put the phone back onto the nightstand. Before I crawled back into bed, I took off my clothes and left them in a pile on the floor. My toe throbbed, as I pulled the covers back and got into bed.

With the covers pulled up to my chin, I wondered what the code could have been on the phone. The pin could have been anything; I thought as I rolled over and snatched a pillow from underneath Trent's head. When he popped up, I closed my eyes tight and pretended to be asleep. He sat up and rested his weight on one of his elbows and I peeked at him out of one of my eyes. Trent then turned over and reached for his phone on the nightstand. With my eyes fully open now that his back was turned, I watched him as he punched in his code.

My eyes involuntarily blinked and I missed seeing him enter the first two numbers of his code. But, I saw the last two numbers, they were 8 and 7. Although I was beyond excited, I remained calm and lay there like I was sleeping. I even added some fake sound effects as If I was snoring. Trent looked my way again for a brief second, and I closed my eyes. After he almost saw me peeking at him, I kept them shut.

From what I could hear, Trent dialed his voicemail and entered a code for that as well. I really wished that I would have been looking, but I didn't want to be caught playing possum. "You have one new voicemail message." I heard, as my eyes darted back and forth under my eyelids. "Hey baby, I wish you didn't have to leave me so early tonight. I can't stop thinking about you. Call me as soon as you get this message."

It took every fiber of my being to stay still as Trent erased the message and got out of the bed. I started to ask where he was going but decided not to as he went into the bathroom and closed the door behind him. I quietly got up and walked over to the bathroom. As I pressed my ear up against the door, I heard him talking on the phone. His voice was small, and he was whispering, but I still heard everything he said loud and clear.

My stomach immediately dropped, and I felt nauseated as I listened. "Diamond, why in the hell would you call my phone in the middle of the night. Have you lost your mind? What if my wife would've answered?" Then there was a long pause before Trent said, "I know that, I can't lose Lyric. I just can't. There's no way that I'm going to do that, we've only been married a week for crying out loud." Then there was another long pause. "Well, that's only because you seduced me. You got what you wanted, didn't you? I was with you for over two hours today. What else do you want from me?"

That was it; I'd heard enough. As I removed my ear from the door, a lump formed in the middle of my throat. Salty tears made their way down my cheeks as I got back in bed. I didn't know what else to do, so I started to cry. At this point, I didn't care if Trent came out and saw me. I was hurt. As silent tears escaped my tear ducts, my pillow grew cold and wet. When my chest began to hurt, I knew that Trent had just broken my heart.

I must admit, I thought that I was in love with someone amazing that would never let me down. I thought that I was in love with someone who took vows to be with me through sickness and health and all that other wedding talk crap. I would have never thought in a million years that Trent was a dirty dog. Without him even knowing it, he'd shown me his true colors, and it only took a week into our marriage for him to do so.

My heart and insides confirmed that tonight was the second most terrible day of my life. It was far worse than finding Latria in Mont's shower, walking in on Dana and Nina having sex, and getting fired from that great paying job at Grant's dentist office. I'd thought he was perfect, but I was wrong. I'd given him all my love, along with my heart and soul. When I heard the bathroom door open I started to confront him, but I decided to wait. As he made himself comfortable on the bed and went back to sleep with no problem, I lay there with dried up tears on my face. When I told Latria about what I'd heard, I knew that she would have an evil plan laid out for Trent in no time. Until then, I was going to beat him at his own game.

4

Return of the Bangles

That very next day I called my mom and asked her to get my bangles out of the safe. I was surprised that she didn't ask me why I wanted them back. Since she wasn't home when I went to pick them up, I let myself in. She said that my bangles would be on the kitchen counter, and they were. When I saw the shiny pieces of gold, I felt butterflies in my stomach. There was a pink sticky note on the counter beside my pile of jewelry. It simply read, "I cleaned them with Dawn dish detergent. Thank me later." I broke the silence with laughter as I looked over at the half empty bottle of dish soap.

Before I touched them, I sat down on one of the leather bar stools and took a deep breath. When I picked up the first bangle, I smiled and remembered that Mont had given it to me. The diamonds sparkled as I held it up. When I looked on the inside of the bangle, I read the words, "Always and forever." I hadn't seen Mont in a long time; I yearned to see him more and more since Trent was acting up and thought about calling him, but didn't follow through with the thought.

While I continued to think about Mont, I picked through the bangles and put on all the ones that he had gotten me first. The next bangles I

35

picked up were the ones that Dana had gotten for me. The one engraved with hearts went on first, and then the others. Next were the bangles from Stanley and Jerry. The rest of the bangles were from a few guys from high school. These didn't have any diamonds, but they were still beautiful.

After I put all the bangles on, I sat perfectly still for a few minutes. When my cell phone rang, it startled me, and I jumped. That very moment, I heard the chant. I hadn't heard this particular jingle in a while, so I moved my arm back and forth again. The familiar noise that I heard reminded me a lot of the bells that people decorated with around Christmas time.

Since I was intrigued by my bangles, I missed the call. As I reached into my purse, I retrieved my cell phone and saw that I had missed a call from Trent. I sucked my teeth as I debated on whether to call him back or not. To tell you the truth, I didn't feel like talking to him. I wasn't sure if I could speak to him without letting him know that I knew about his mistress.

I decided not to call him back, as I picked up a pen off of the counter and responded to mom's note. I wrote, "Thanks mom, you're the best." When I put the pen back down, my phone rang again after I looked at the screen, I saw that it was my mom.

"Hey Mom."

"Hi, darling. Did you go to the house yet?"

"Yes. I'm here now."

"Great, can you boil a dozen eggs before you leave? I have Bible study tonight, and I don't have anything to take for refreshments," she stated.

"Yes. I'll make them for you. That way you won't have to rush home. I'll bring them to the church if you need me to."

"Thanks pumpkin, I really would appreciate that."

"No problem at all and thanks for cleaning my bangles too," I added while I reached into the cabinet for a pot.

Before Mom and I were done talking, she told me that I had received some mail and that it was in the letter rack in the foyer. After we ended the call, I decided to start with the deviled eggs before I checked my mail. I maneuvered around the kitchen like I did when I was younger. I opened the refrigerator and got the eggs, mayo, mustard, and relish. When I closed the refrigerator, I heard the jingle of my bangles again, and the sound didn't irritate me. Next, I carefully dropped the eggs into the water, turned an egg-shaped timer on, and went into the living room.

Everybody Hates Chris was playing when I turned on the television. Mom loved that show; I secretly think that she had a crush on Julius. While I watched Chris get into all sorts of predicaments, the doorbell sounded, "Just a second," I yelled as I made my way to the door. To my surprise, Boogie was standing there. He was wearing an Army uniform that complimented his brown skin.

"Oh my God. Boogie," I yelled as I opened the screen door.

"Hey, I've only been home about an hour, when I looked out of the window and saw your car I rushed over," Boogie said as he leaned in to give me a hug.

"I heard you got married; my mom told me. I'm sorry I missed the wedding."

"That's alright; I knew you were serving our country."

"Mom has plenty of pictures in here if you have the time, I'd love to show you some."

"I've got all the time in the world," he replied as he closed the front door.

While Boogie and I caught up, I gave him a good look over. He was so handsome, he had always been a good looking guy, but something about him was different. I could tell that he had matured while he was away. The way he sat told me that. He didn't slouch anymore. He sat up straight and looked me in my eyes as we talked.

"Lyric, you looked amazing in your wedding dress. That Trent, is one lucky guy," he said, as he turned the pages in the album.

"Yeah, he is. I just wish that he knew that," I responded, as I sat back on the couch.

"Uh-oh, what's going on Lyric?"

"Boogie you just got here, the last thing I want to do is bury you in my troubles."

"Lyric, you know we go way back. Even though I've been gone, and I've changed a little; I'm still the same Boogie."

"Well, I recently found out that Trent has been talking to a woman by the name of Diamond."

"Damn, you guys haven't even been married for a month yet, and he's already messing up. Jesus take the wheel," he teased.

"I don't know what I'm going to do. I want to confront him, but a part of me is thirsty for payback," I confessed, as I jingled my arm back and forth.

"You and those bangles," Boogie said, as he shook his head from side to side."

That's why I'm here. I came to pick up my bangles. Believe it or not, I stopped wearing them for a while. Look at my wedding pictures," I said, as I pointed to my arm in the picture.

"Damn, you're really serious."

"Yep, I gave up my bangles for Trent but since he wants to be a two-timing dog, I'm going to give him a dose of his own medicine. That's why the bangles are back; I feel sexier than ever since I put them on too..."

That was all I had a chance to say before Boogie cut me off. He stammered a bit before he blew my mind.

"I hope you don't take this the wrong way, but maybe you should give me a try. I know you better than Trent and Mont," he said, as he looked into my eyes.

"Boogie are you serious?"

"Yeah, I always thought that you were beautiful, I just wasn't bold enough to say anything until now. Being in the military has changed me, and I know that I can keep you happy. All you have to do is give me a chance; I won't tell a single soul. Since your old man is acting up, you should consider it."

I was totally speechless. I couldn't believe that Boogie had been sweet on me for all these years. Without thinking, I leaned over and kissed him smack dab on the lips. He was shocked, but reacted by kissing me back. I can't lie; it felt good. I wanted to go further with him, but I just couldn't. He was like a family member to me, and this would not only be gross, but awkward if I continued to make out with him.

After kissing him for a few more seconds, my body temperature rose a few degrees. I knew I had to back away before I did something I regretted. As much as my body wanted Boogie and his new Army buff body all over me, I stopped kissing him and slid to the other end of the couch. I blushed, as I started to speak.

"Damn, I'm sorry, I shouldn't have kissed you. As much as I would like to give you a chance, I just can't. I can't ruin a perfectly good friendship. I love you too much as a friend to let something sexual happen between us. Do you understand where I'm coming from?"

"Yeah, I understand. I'd hate to lose our friendship too. You're right. It really wouldn't be worth it. I think I'd better go."

I gave him one final hug before he left. As he walked down the sidewalk, I wanted to call him back, but something deep down inside wouldn't let me. The kiss that Boogie and I shared today would be the only kiss he would ever taste from my lips. I hope he enjoyed it as much as I did.

After I closed the door, I licked my lips and saw the letter rack full of mail. I grabbed the envelopes and sat back down in front of the television. All the mail from my old apartment came to my mom's house. I had it forwarded because Trent and I hadn't bought our house yet, and I wasn't sure what our new address would be.

As I opened envelope after envelope of bills that I'd already paid, I saw an envelope that was only addressed to me. It looked to be a personal letter, and I'm sure that it wasn't a bill at all. When I pulled out the paper, I immediately started reading:

Thank you for dining at the Red Rooster. We appreciate your business. Please accept this coupon to use the next time you visit our restaurant. If you have any questions, comments, or concerns, please don't hesitate to give us a call at 808-699-0313.

This was very strange. However, this was the restaurant that Trent and I had eaten at while we were in Hawaii. The crazy thing was that I didn't remember giving them my address at all. *"How in the hell did they get all of my personal information?"* I wondered, as my mind thought back to the day that Trent and I'd eaten at the restaurant. I remembered Jason checking my ID when I ordered the daiquiri, and then the lightbulb in my head went off. I think that this was Jason's way of reaching out to me. At that very moment, the timer in the kitchen started to buzz.

While the timer in the kitchen continued to make an irritating buzzing sound, I looked over the coupon and thank you letter again. It was definitely homemade, no professional printing company should have been paid for doing such a crappy job on a flyer and a coupon. Before I called the number at the bottom of the flyer, I cut the timer off and poured the hot water off of the boiled eggs.

Since I was there alone, I dialed the number and used the speaker function, so I could start making the deviled eggs. The phone rang four times before I heard his baritone voice.

"Hello," he answered.

"Hi, Jason, it's Lyric," I said, with a little giggle in my voice.

"Lyric, I've been waiting for you to call me. I sent you that fake flyer and coupon the same day I met you," he confessed.

"How did you know that I would call?" I asked, as my bangles jingled while peeling the shells off of the eggs.

"Oh, I knew. I could tell that you were feeling me, I wanted to ask you for your number so bad, but your man came back."

"Well, he's not around right now, and I've got time to talk. So, what's up?" I asked seductively.

"You're what's up. Since I saw you last week, I couldn't stop thinking about you, and I'm glad that you called me."

"That's sweet, but can I ask you a question real quick?"

"Sure baby girl. Ask me anything," he said.

"How did you remember my information on my license?"

"Easy, I have a photographic memory," he bragged.

"Really?" I asked with a high pitched voice.

"Nah. I scribbled it down on a napkin, as soon as I went to get your drink order," he laughed.

I laughed too, as I mixed the egg yolks together with the remainder of the ingredients.

"On a serious note, though I'm going to be in Virginia next month, and I would love to see you. Do you think you can make that happen?"

"I'm sure I could work something out." I replied and then added, "The number that I'm calling you from is my cell. Save it and call me a few days before you fly out of Hawaii."

"Sure thing, only I'd like to hear your voice sooner than next month, though. Is it possible that I can call you tomorrow or can you call me?"

As my mind quickly thought about Trent and the conversation he had with Diamond last night in the bathroom, I responded to Jason in no time.

"Sure sexy, text me first, and I'll let you know if it's okay to call, and don't call me in the middle of the night. You've got to remember that we're in different time zones."

"Yes ma'am. That bossy shit turns me on."

I talked to Jason until I was about to leave my mom's house. With my hands full, I couldn't close the door behind me, so I had to make two trips. After I made sure the entry door was locked, I walked to my car and got in. When I started the engine and put the car in reverse, I heard a text message notification. I wanted to see who it was from, but I knew that I had to get these eggs to mom at the church.

When I drove down the street a little more, I saw Boogie. He was outside of his mother's house, getting his luggage out of his trunk. I blew the horn at him when I drove by and had to do a double-take because he'd taken his shirt off. "DAMN," I said, as I slowed down and attempted to drive and look in the rear view mirror at the same time. Seeing him with no shirt on made me have a change of heart. I wished I would have let him show me what he was working with and even thought about calling him later.

As I made left and right turns through the city, I approached the flower shop that I always got Melody's flowers from. Even though I was in a time crunch, I quickly parallel parked and got out of the car. As I entered the shop, I was greeted by my old friend behind the counter.

"Flowers for Melody today my love?" She asked.

"No ma'am, not today. I'd like a dozen pink roses for my mom; I'll come back and get Melody's flowers sometime soon," I replied.

"One dozen of pink roses coming up," she announced, as she walked to the back of the flower shop.

"Thank you for the beautiful flowers at the wedding. You did an amazing job. I forgot to call you when I got home from the honeymoon."

"Sweetie, it was my pleasure, I just wish I could have been there. So how was the honeymoon?" She asked as she wiggled her eyebrows up and down.

"We had a blast, and we really enjoyed one another."

"You look like you're glowing? Are you pregnant?" She asked as she arranged the roses in a glass vase.

"I better not be. I'm not ready for more kids. Tia is more than a handful. I don't know what I'd do if I got pregnant this early in my marriage," I revealed.

"You'd love the child; that's what you would do. I just know you're going to be a good mother. I can feel it in my bones."

"You think so?" I asked as I handed her two crisp twenty dollar bills.

She didn't respond, she only took the money and smiled.

When I got back to the car, I couldn't stop thinking about what my old friend said. Did she know something I didn't know? I had no clue, but I had to deliver these eggs and flowers to my mom fast. After I drove through three green lights, I saw the church. The parking lot was full, I knew that bible study had already started. I didn't want to go inside of the church, but mom wasn't answering her phone. "Shit," I said out loud before I covered my mouth. I'd forgotten that I was on a church ground.

The moment I heard singing coming from inside of the church, I knew that bible study had started. So grabbed the platter of eggs, along with the flowers and made my way to the reception hall. To my surprise, the door was cracked. As I entered, I saw one of my mom's church friends. She was talking on the phone that was mounted on a beige wall. I didn't feel like talking to her because she didn't know when to stop talking. I only waved and walked by with the eggs and flowers.

After I set the flowers on the counter and put the eggs in the refrigerator, I went back to close the door to the reception hall. By that time Mrs. Blabber Mouth had ended her call, and was looking in my direction. I wanted to say another cuss word, but I resisted the urge and held it in.

"I haven't seen you in a while. How have you been?" She asked, as she sat down and pulled a chair out for me to sit in.

"I've been great," I answered, as I leaned down and gave her a hug. "I'm sorry that I couldn't make the wedding. My oldest daughter had a baby, and I had to go to Florida,"

"That's okay," I said as I thought about the invitation list for the wedding. I didn't remember her being invited.

As I resisted the urge to sit in the chair, I leaned on the back of it and listened to her go on and on. She told me about her husband needing back surgery, the bald spot her poodle had, and that she needed a root canal. I stood there in silence and wondered how I was going to get away from her. Just then my cell phone buzzed, and I took it out of my back pocket. It buzzed again as I entered my security code and checked my new messages.

While I fumbled with my phone, I only heard bits and pieces of the rest of Mrs. Blabbermouth's conversation. When I saw that the text was from Jason, I opened it and read, "Hey, send me a picture. I'm going to send you one now." I closed the text and immediately opened the image that he had sent. My eyes almost popped out of my head when I saw the picture. Jason was in the shower with a very muscular body and a semi-erect penis.

I knew that I couldn't carry on a conversation any longer after I'd seen that.

"Can you please make sure that my mom gets her flowers?" I asked as I pointed to the roses sitting on the counter.

"Sure dear," she responded.

"Thank you, I wish I could stay and talk, but I've got to go." I mumbled as I stumbled out the reception hall door.

"It was good talking to you Lyric, I'll tell your mother that you bought the eggs too," she said.

My knees felt weak as I opened my car door and sat down in the driver's seat. I looked at the picture again before I sent it to Latria with the caption, "THIS IS JASON." Not even ten seconds later, my cell phone rang. I knew it was Latria because she has her very own ringtone. I answered, "Girl you're not going to believe this," I yelled as I started the engine and backed out of the parking space.

5

An Eye for an Eye

By the time I'd gotten to Latria's, I'd already told her about picking up my bangles from mom's house, Jason and the fake flyer, Trent and his late night conversation with Diamond, and Boogie coming on to me. After hearing about all of those things that I'd encountered in less than a 24-hour time frame, Latria had our drinks poured when I arrived. I hadn't been over to her place for a while, and I noticed that she'd painted the kitchen a sage color and hung new curtains. I kicked my shoes off at the front door and went to sit on my favorite couch.

When Latria bounced around the corner, she handed me a drink, and I took a sip. She knew how to make a mean Pina Colada. Before she sat down, she took off her shoes as well and sat on the other end of the couch.

"So what are you going to do?" She asked.

"About Trent, Boogie, or Jason?" I replied.

"I think we should handle Trent first," She said as she took a drink.

"Okay, now that we know that he's cheating, what am I supposed to do?"

"Lyric, there are a few things you can do. You can confront him and stay, confront him and leave, don't confront him at all and collect more evidence for a divorce, or you can give him a taste of his own medicine."

"You've got a good point. I'm not going to confront him yet, I'd like to give him a taste of his own medicine first," I chuckled, as I shook my bangles at Latria.

"Girl, he's in trouble now. Those bangles mean business. So, are you going to go back to doing all of those scandalous things that you used to do?" She asked as she dug into her oversized purse.

"Well, I know that I'm going to screw Jason, just as soon as his plane touches down in Virginia. As for Boogie, I don't think I'm going to pursue him after I rejected him already. I am very curious about Diamond, though. I would like to know where they met and how often he's been with her."

"Honey, trust me, you don't want to know about the personal stuff because you'll never be able to get it out of your head," Latria said, as she continued to dig in her purse.

"What on earth are you looking for?" I asked as she pulled out some crumpled papers.

"There are 36 licensed and permitted drivers in this county with the legal name of Diamond. This is a list of addresses, phone numbers, and other personal information from the database at the DMV. The ages range from 16-47, I think it would be safe to say that we can go ahead and strike a line through the 16-and-17 year olds," she said, as she took a huge sip from her glass.

"That's why you're my girl. I knew I could count on you," I cheered from the other end of the sofa. "So what if her name isn't Diamond. What if it's just a nickname?" I asked as I settled down.

"That's why you need to get her phone number."

"I don't know if I'll be able to do that because Trent has a pin lock on his phone. Last night when I tried to look at his phone, I couldn't get in. After trying my birthday, Tia's birthday, and his birthday, I didn't have any luck. All I know for sure is that the pin contains four digits and that the last two numbers are 87," I sighed.

"If the pin is a birthday, whose could it be? Who was born in 1987?" Latria asked as she finished her drink.

"I don't know, but I'll find out because I've got to get inside of that phone."

"Oh, while you're here, let me hear that message that Mont left you again," she said, as I grabbed my phone.

"Let's look at that picture of Jason again first, isn't he dangerously delicious!" I declared, as I slid closer and we both stared at the picture.

"Damn, I need to go to Hawaii. Does he have a brother or cousin that at least resembles him?"

"I'm not sure, I could ask him for you if you want me to," I answered, as I punched in the code for my voicemail and put the phone on speaker. Just then, Mont's voice filled the air:

"This is the last time I'm going to call you, so you don't have to worry about changing your number. I just wanted you to know that I couldn't sleep, and I was up thinking about you. You're supposed to be my wife, and you know that. You were supposed to be making love to me tonight. I don't think I'll ever get over this, Lyric. I know I said that I would stay away from you but I can't. You're the first thing on my mind when I wake up and the last person I think about before I go to sleep every night. It doesn't matter who I lay beside; I won't be satisfied until it's you. I still love you and want you even though you belong to someone else. I hope Trent treats you right, if he doesn't, just know that I will always be here waiting for you to return to my arms. I love you."

Latria and I listened to Mont's message again, and I saved it before I ended the voicemail call.

"He said he'd be waiting for you with open arms if Trent were to mess up. Maybe you should give him another try. You know, if things don't work out between you and Trent," she said.

"You're right Latria. I just may do that. I know that he'll be happy to hear from me. He's always happy to hear from his favorite girl," I replied with a smirk.

After we had another drink, we went through the list of names from the DMV. As we tried to narrow the list down, an hour passed. We realized that this was a crazy idea and that there was no way we would be able to find out if the right Diamond was on this list. Before I left Latria's house, she told me that I needed to break the code on Trent's phone tonight. "I'll try," I replied as I gathered my things and headed out the door.

On the way home, Trent called me and asked if I could pick up Tia from his mom's house. After agreeing to do so, I made a U turn in the middle of the road and picked up Tia. When we got home, Trent's car was in the yard. If he was already home, I wondered why he couldn't get Tia. While the wheels in my head turned, my head began to ache. On top of that, Tia had fallen asleep, and I had to carry her inside.

When I got to the porch, I struggled to hold Tia's limp body and unlock the entry door. As I tried to turn the doorknob, the door opened, and Trent reached out for Tia. My body still felt weighed down immediately after he relieved my body of the extra 40 pounds. I don't know what it was, but it seemed as if Tia weighed more when she was asleep. "Thank you," I said as I looked at him standing in his pajamas.

As he carried Tia to her bedroom, I watched him carefully. The back of his thin t-shirt was damp, so that meant he must've just showered. Before he could come back, I quickly went into our bedroom and looked to see if there was steam on the bathroom mirror and there was.

"Are you cooking tonight or are we ordering in?" He asked.

"Let's order in," I insisted, as I looked around the bedroom. When I saw his phone on the nightstand, I walked over and picked it up.

"Here, you can order whatever you want. I'm going to take a shower."

After Trent took his phone out of my hand, he sat on the bed and pretended to watch television. I thought I was being slick by taking my time, but I guess Trent knew what I was up to because he didn't touch his phone until my back was turned. As he ordered a pizza and hot wings. I sucked my teeth under my breath and went into the bathroom.

While in the shower, I remembered that I'd never sent Jason a picture. I was glad that I remembered because I hadn't deleted his image yet and I needed to before Trent saw it. With damp hands, I looked at Jason's naked image one last time and deleted it. After I deleted the picture, I dried off and rubbed baby oil all over my body. When everything was super shiny, I snapped a few quick pictures and sent them to Jason.

As I waited for him to respond, I put the phone near the sink and began my nightly regimen. Just as I picked up the cotton balls, my phone lit up. Jason responded to my nude picture in no time. "I'm in love," he replied in the text message. I laughed quietly as I responded, "No, you're not. You're in lust." "What took you so long to respond? Can I call you now?" He messaged back. "I was at church when you sent that nude picture. I couldn't just go to the bathroom and take dirty pictures in the Lord's house. I can't talk now; my husband is home. I'll call you tomorrow." I replied back as I sat down on the toilet.

While I waited for Jason to respond, the bathroom doorknob started to wiggle. My heart dropped, and I fumbled with my phone. "I forgot to take my vitamin. Bring me one out of the medicine cabinet whenever you come out," Trent said, as he wiggled the handle again. I didn't want him to be suspicious of what I was doing in the bathroom, and I quickly powered my phone off and opened the locked door. "Come in, you can get it yourself," I said as I put on my robe and slid my phone into the pocket.

As he entered the sweet-smelling bathroom, he said, "It sure smells good in here." "It's a new fragrance from Bath and Body Works," I chimed. When I started dabbing my face with the wet cotton balls, Trent got his vitamin out of the bottle and chewed it up. He looked at me suspiciously before he left the bathroom, and didn't bother closing the door behind him.

After I finished up my regimen, I stepped into my closet and powered my phone back on. Jason messaged me another picture; this one wasn't a nude. It was a picture of his face, it looked like he was at work. He looked so good I wanted to kiss the screen of my phone. I didn't want to delete this picture permanently, so I sent the image to my email. After getting rid of the picture, I read the two new text messages that he sent. One read, "Sweet dreams," and the other read, "I'll be waiting for your call tomorrow."

When I left my closet, I noticed that there was an extra body in my bed.

"I can't sleep Mommy Lyric. Can I sleep with you and Daddy?" I looked at Trent to see that he was already asleep. I was going to let him answer her question but he couldn't, so I did.

"Umm, how would you like it if I sleep with you in your bed?" I asked, as her face lit up.

"Yay," Tia yelled, as she jumped out of the bed.

With her yelling and bouncing on the bed, I was surprised that Trent didn't wake up. Before leaving the room, I grabbed the box of pizza. Tia and I finished the box off at the kitchen counter I put her back to bed.

We walked hand in hand to her bedroom, and the first thing I saw was Trent and Anna's wedding picture. It was leaning on the wall near Tia's play kitchen. *I wondered if Trent cheated on Anna,* I thought to myself as Tia and I got comfortable on her bed. While Tia talked about cartoons and Disney Land, I couldn't stop myself from looking at the picture of Trent and Anna. If she'd lived, I wondered where I would have been at this very moment.

Would Trent and I even know each other? Would Trent have been one of my sugar daddies? Could I've been in a relationship with Mont or Dana or would I still be on the road with Know Betta? While I was thinking about the way my life would have been with Mont or Dana, I noticed that Tia had stopped talking. She'd fallen asleep that fast.

Even though she was sleep, I stayed in her room. I stared at the ceiling and continued to think. When my eyes could no longer stay open, I fell asleep holding onto one of Tia's teddy bears. I didn't know how long I was asleep, and I wasn't sure if my dream of Anna or a warm sensation on my back woke me up. I jumped up only to find out that Tia had wet the bed. She'd not only wet the bed, but she'd wet me too.

The back of my robe was saturated with urine. Tia was still asleep and didn't know that she was lying in a puddle of pee. I was immediately grossed out and headed to my room. With Trent still sleeping, I took a shower and put on one of his t-shirts. I then got in the bed and tried to remember the dream that I'd had about Anna. No matter how hard I thought, I couldn't remember the dream. As I pulled the covers up to my chin, I felt drowsy and drifted off into a light sleep. Just as I closed my eyes, they flew back open and the thought of Trent's security code.

Maybe it's Anna's birthday; I said to myself as I crawled out of the bed and got Trent's phone off of his nightstand. Just like last night, blue light was flashing. I wondered what type of message Diamond left Trent tonight. I laughed an evil laugh inside of my head as I took the phone into the bathroom and started punching in codes. I knew that Anna's birthday was in July, so I punched in codes like 7187, 7287, 7387, and so on. After I punched in the code 7787, the phone unlocked.

I couldn't believe that I'd figured out the code. I was so happy that I wanted to tell Latria and planned on sending her a text message as soon as I got back to my phone. After doing a soundless victory dance, I checked Trent's call log and saw Diamond's name and number several times. It even looked like he'd talked to her while I was in the shower last night. *"That dirty dog,"* I thought to myself as I searched for something to copy down her phone number.

After thinking long and hard, I remembered that a pack of eyeliner pencils were underneath my sink. When I opened the cabinet, I searched for the pencils and saw that they were inside of a plastic package. I wondered if it was worth the risk of waking Trent up and decided to go back into the bedroom and get my cell phone. I quietly crept to my side of the bed and snatched my phone off of the nightstand. When I returned to the bathroom, I took pictures of his call log and all the text messages. I almost dropped the phone when I saw an image of a brown-skinned lady wearing a white skin tight dress. That was the first time that I'd seen Diamond.

She was very attractive, and she didn't look like she had on any makeup. On a scale of 1-10, her body was a 9. Diamond's hair was jet black and cut into a blunt bob with a bang. I wasn't sure if it was a wig, weave, or her natural hair. I honestly couldn't tell. I don't think I'd ever seen her before. As I continued to look at the picture, I looked at the background, and it looked like the picture was taken in Trent's office at the funeral home. My heart began to race as I continued to look through the rest of the digital images. When I'd seen a selfie type picture of Trent and Diamond kissing; I'd seen enough. I figured the images I'd taken pictures of were enough for tonight. Since I had the code I could check his phone anytime I wanted to.

When I put Trent's phone back on his nightstand, I was sweating because I was just that mad. I knew that my blood pressure was sky high, and I prayed that I wouldn't smother Trent with a pillow as he slept peacefully next to me. While I tried to go back to sleep, I tossed, and I turned. Then I realized that I wouldn't be able to go back to sleep, so I got up. After I put on a fresh robe, I grabbed my phone off of the nightstand and went into the living room.

I wanted a snack, but the way my stomach was feeling, I decided not to eat anything. After turning the television on, I plopped down on the couch. While I channel surfed, I felt my eyes begin to water. I knew the tears were coming, so I let them fall freely. I didn't wipe my face in my robe or anything. The tears just dripped down my chin and fell onto the front of my robe. After I was all cried out, I went to the kitchen and drank three shots of vodka. Then I wiped my face with a paper towel after I remembered that I hadn't sent Latria the evidence from Trent's phone.

After I went back to the living room, I started sending Latria the messages from Trent's phone. I started to call her, but I knew that she had to be at work early in the morning. After I sent the last piece of evidence, Mont crossed my mind and I listened to his voicemail message. I wondered what he was doing at this very moment and was tempted to call him. Could he possibly be thinking about me? I wondered as I dialed his number privately. I just wanted to hear his voice that was all. As soon as he answered, I was going to hang up. That's what I told myself, but when I heard his voice all the feelings I had for him came rushing back instantaneously.

"Hello," he said groggily.

I started to hang up, but when he said "Hello," again, I responded.

"Hey, are you asleep?"

"Lyric, is this you?" He asked.

I quietly said, "Yeah, it's me," then there was a long pause followed by a question.

"Do you still love me?" He asked.

I wanted to lie, but I didn't, there was no need because he knew the truth.

"Yes. I love you," I said as I let out a deep breath.

"That's all I wanted to hear. Are you alright?" He questioned.

"No, I'm not alright. I found out that Trent is cheating on me," I sobbed.

"Damn, have the two of you even been married a week?"

"I know. It's terrible isn't it?"

"Yeah, that's pretty messed up," Mont confessed.

"So what were you doing? I don't want to get you into any trouble with your girlfriend."

"You're good, she's sleeping. I wore her ass out," he laughed, and I got jealous.

"I don't want to hear that shit," I spat, as I looked around to make sure that I was the only person in the living room.

Trent had already made me mad, and I didn't want to hear any slick talk from Mont.

"I'm sorry," he whispered.

"That's alright, I don't want to hear about your sex life. I already know you can put it down in the bedroom. I don't want to hear about you getting it on with anybody else. You got that?" I said.

"Yeah, I got it sweet lips. Hey, do you think that we can meet up one day this week? I'd love to see you and I promise that I will keep my hands to myself," he said.

"I might be able to make that happen. I would love to see you too. I'm going to call you tomorrow after Trent goes to work if that's alright."

"Yeah, call me whenever and I'll answer. I'll talk to you tomorrow. I Love you."

"I Love you too," I replied before I hung up the phone.

"Wait a minute, did I just tell Mont that I loved him?" I thought, as I turned the television off and headed back to bed. I sure did, but there wasn't a damn thing I could do about it now. I shook my head and looked at the clock in the room; it was a little after five in the morning. Trent would have to get up in less than two hours. As I settled in the bed,

the warm blankets welcomed me and I fell into a magnificent dream about Mont. We were hugging, kissing, and holding hands. It felt so real that I didn't want to wake up when I heard Trent's alarm clock going off.

The irritating sound made my skin crawl as I looked around for Trent only to find that he was nowhere in sight. "Trent cut your alarm off," I yelled as I heard the bathroom door open. "Oh sorry baby, I thought I'd turned the alarm off before I went into the bathroom," he said, as he pushed the button on the alarm clock. When he went back into the bathroom to gargle, I checked my phone and I had over a dozen text messages.

Latria had called me three times already and sent nine text messages. The other messages were from Jason and Mont. Jason's message read, "Good morning beautiful." Mont's two messages read, "Can we meet today," and "Please." I sat up with a smile on my face and responded to Mont's text, "Sure, we can meet today. I'll call you with the place and time in an hour or so." Mont's response was a smiley face. While Trent got ready to leave. I lay in bed with a huge smile on my face, and thought about what I was going to wear for my meeting with Mont.

Trent looked very handsome when he came out of the bathroom. He bent down and gave me a kiss on the cheek before he left.

"Can your mom watch Tia today?"

"She should be able to, just call her. You know she doesn't mind," he said.

"Okay, I'll do that," I replied as he left. I was so overjoyed that I'd almost forgot that Tia pissed the bed and needed a bath before I took her anywhere.

While I cooked breakfast, I let Tia play in the tub. I started to call Latria while I waited for Tia to finish, but I only responded to her text messages and told her to call me on her lunch break. I didn't want Tia to repeat anything that I told Latria, so I thought it would be best if we talked later. I would never underestimate the intelligence of a 4 year-old, well at least not this 4-year old.

After she was squeaky clean, I dressed her and put her linen in the washing machine. Then we ate our waffles and eggs. While I cleaned the mess up in the bathroom, she watched television. Mont was heavy on my mind, now that I was finished cleaning. After sending him a message, I called Trent's mom to see if she could watch Tia. When she said that she could, I smiled ear to ear and told her that I would be there within the next hour. As I got dressed, I thought long and hard about where I would meet Mont. Could I meet him at a bar or the mall parking lot in the next town over? I didn't know; I guess we would discuss that after I dropped Tia off.

6

A Touch of Love

My bangles jingled as I shut the entry door to my mother-in-law's house. I'd just dropped Tia off, and I was heading back to my car when my cell phone rang.

"Girl, where are you meeting Mont?"

"Why aren't you working?" I asked, with a giggle.

"It's slow at the DMV today. I had to call because your text messages were about to give me a heart attack. Why was it taking you so long to answer?"

"I was cooking, giving Tia a bath, doing laundry, getting ready, and driving," I replied.

"Oh, you were multitasking," Latria joked and then added, "Way to go on breaking the code. I knew it was going to be something easy."

As Latria rambled on, I started the engine and put her on speakerphone.

"I can't believe that hoochie was in his office with that skin tight dress on," she chimed as I sent Mont a text message.

When he responded that we could meet at a coffee house about twenty minutes away, I sent an ok response and headed his way. I couldn't believe that the DMV, wasn't busy but I was thankful as I pulled into the parking lot of the coffee house.

Just as I was about to end the call with Latria, she said, "I found Diamond in the system. Her last name is Murphy. I've got her address and everything. She was on the list that we had yesterday, I knew if you found out what her phone number was, we would find out who this hussy is."

"Girl, you've got to be kidding me. You've had her information the entire time we've been on the phone, and you're just now telling me. You're fired," I said with a laugh.

"Yeah right, I'm not fired because you'll need this vital piece of information," she boasted.

"What vital information?"

"Her work phone number," she said.

"What? I'm going to call there now, what's the number?" I asked as I hooked up a three-way call.

After I entered a block code, I dialed the number. Latria and I were quiet as church mice. When I heard someone pick up the phone and say, "Diamond's Gems and Jewels. Diamond speaking, how may I help you?" Shit! I couldn't think of anything to say, and I started to hang up. That's when Latria disguised her voice and said, "Good morning ma'am. Are you interested in any fresh, frozen shrimp?" "Excuse me sir, this is a business that sells fine jewelry. Please don't call soliciting again," Diamond said in an irritated voice. Then she hung up, and we burst out laughing.

"Did she say that was a jewelry store?" Latria asked in a high pitched voice.

"Yep," I said, as I looked at my ring. "I think this is where Trent got my wedding ring. I knew that he had to have some input from a woman about this ring, and I was right."

"We should go down there one day; I'm going to get the address for Diamond's Gems and Jewels on my lunch break. I'll think of something, but I've got to go. An ass load of people just walked through the door."

"Alright, I'll talk to you later," I said before I hung up.

"So Miss. Diamond Murphy owns a jewelry store," I thought to myself as I looked in the mirror on the visor. *"What does that bitch have that I don't?"* I said out loud, as I slammed the visor up to the ceiling. I looked damn good, and I knew that I was a better catch than this Diamond chick. After primping in the mirror, I looked around the parking lot, but I didn't see Mont's Porsche. Instead of sitting alone in the car and making myself upset, I decided that I should go inside and grab a table. The coffee house was small, but the parking lot was jam packed.

I wondered if this would be a good place to meet Mont, considering that there were so many people inside. But all we were doing was having coffee, cocoa, or whatever the hell they served at this place. As I calmed down, my breathing slowed, and I got out of the car. On the way to the coffee house, several men turned their heads and watched me sashay inside. My skin tight jeans and low cut blouse caught their attention and had them tuned in. I knew that they couldn't resist looking, and I hoped that Mont couldn't resist either.

My soft brown curls, desirable fragrance, and red lipstick had the men hypnotized. Some even stared at me after I sat down at a table near the back of the coffee house. Not even a minute after I'd made my grand entrance, I saw Mont walk through the door. Now it was his turn to make his entrance. Even though it had only been a few months, I absolutely couldn't take my eyes off him. He looked damn good, and my mouth watered. As the soft jazz played and the incense burned, he looked around.

When he saw me, a small smile spread across his face, and he headed in my direction. Dressed in a form-fitting heather gray suit with a black dress shirt and matching leather shoes, he strutted his stuff too. A few ladies looked his way and had a look of lust in their eyes until they saw me watching them. As he got closer to our small table, I tried to think of how I should greet him. Should I stand up and give him a hug, stay seated and smile, or give him my hand to kiss? With only a few moments left to decide, I made my mind up to stand and give him a hug.

"Lyric, it's so good to see you," he said, as I stood up to hug him. When his warm arms wrapped around me, the world stood still. Being buried in his arms made my mind wander to the naughty times that we once shared. His scent was the same, and I wanted to melt into him. When he finally let me go, I kissed him on his cheek. That definitely wasn't a part of the greeting plan, but I did it. I knew he liked it because of the look on his handsome face.

After we both sat down, I looked around to see if anyone I knew was in the coffee house. I didn't see any familiar faces in the crowd, and I was thankful. Could you imagine getting a call out of the blue saying that someone saw your wife kissing another man in public? That would've been terrible. I had to control my emotions while I was out in public with Mont. Maybe people thought that we were cousins or possibly sister and brother. The bottom line was that I had to control myself.

"It's good to see you too," I said while the voice inside my head continued to talk to me.

"Did you want a drink?" He asked.

"Sure," I responded, as I read the menu.

I ended up ordering a peppermint Frappuccino. When Mont came back with our drinks, he introduced me to his drink and asked if I wanted a sip. After taking a sip from my cup and a sip of his. We ended up trading drinks; Mont ordered an Ice toasted graham latte, and it was very delicious.

Just as I took a big gulp of the sweet beverage, he asked, "Can I hold your hand?"

"I don't think that would be a wise thing to do in here. Suppose one of Trent's associates saw us," I said, as I nervously looked around.

"Well, how about we go somewhere where no one can see us," he suggested, with a seductive look.

The bangles on my arm sounded as I grabbed my drink off of the table and got up. With Mont close on my heels, I knew that the guys from earlier were watching. They just weren't staring quite as hard because they thought that Mont was my lover.

In the parking lot, Mont and I got into his Porsche. When he started the engine, Avant's, *Read Your Mind* made its way through the speakers. The smooth voice of the singer gave me chills. Then Mont took my hand and held it gently. As he backed up out of the parking space with one hand on the steering wheel, I looked in the direction of my car. I wondered if we were going to his house or a nearby hotel. My question was answered when he pulled onto the interstate and took the next exit ramp.

The signs for lodging had four hotels listed Staybridge Suites, Holiday Inn, Candlewood Suites, and Best Western. My heart thumped as the sweet music continued to play. After holding Mont's hand, I was ready to give it up. I couldn't wait to be alone with him in that hotel room. "Are you alright?" He asked. "Yeah. I'm good," I responded, as we pulled into the Candlewood Suites parking lot. When he turned the engine off, I unbuckled my seat belt and we both opened our car doors.

As we walked inside the hotel, I sat in the lobby while Mont waited in line to get a room. I watched everyone as they came and went. When he motioned for me to come on, I got up and followed him to the elevator. "We're on the second floor," he announced as he pressed the number 2 button on the wall of the elevator. "Okay," I replied with a nervous smile. A loud "ding" went off as the elevator doors opened on the second floor.

Mont and I got off to an empty hallway and walked until we reached room 212.

After he swiped the card in the door, a green light flashed, and we entered the room. The set up was usual. A king size bed, television, microwave, mini fridge, small table, vanity area, and full bath. I started taking off my shoes, and Mont did the same. When I unbuttoned my pants and slid them down over my hips, Mont watched me. I gave him a little smile and took off my blouse next. "Come here," he whispered, as he reached out for me. I walked over and embraced him. His lips tasted like the peppermint drink he drank back at the coffee house.

Then we fell onto the bed and slowly grinded on one another until we couldn't take it anymore. As he fondled my private areas, my thoughts ran wild. My bangles clinked as I reached down and guided his thick erection into my hot wetness. *"Damn, I don't ever remember it feeling this good,"* I thought to myself as I wrapped my legs around his lean body. I felt so good; I felt like drooling. I called for Mont as he slowly savored every plunge into my juicy love box until my cell phone rang.

He stopped moving for a moment, and I stopped moaning.

"I should get that; it might be you know who," I said, as I rolled my eyes.

"No, I think that you know who can wait," he said, with a serious face, then he started to grind slowly against me again.

Just as I was about to climax the phone went off again, and I got worried.

"Mont, I really need to get that. Something may be wrong with Tia,"

"Alright," he said as he withdrew himself.

Then I quickly turned over and reached inside of my purse for the ringing cell phone.

"Hello," I answered as I saw Trent's name on the screen of the phone.

"Hey baby, I was calling to see how your day was going?"

Before I could answer Trent, Mont entered my wetness from behind, and I almost screamed in Trent's ear.

"Oh, it's going good baby," I said to Trent.

Meanwhile, Mont continued to give it to me slowly as I wrapped up the conversation with Trent.

"Are you cooking tonight?" Trent asked.

"Yes! I'm going to cook tonight. Anything you want in particular?" I said in an almost whiny voice.

"How about spaghetti?" He suggested.

"Yeah, baby. I'll cook it with lots of sausage and bell peppers, just the way you like," I added.

"I should be home by 8:30," he replied.

"Okay, I'll see you then," I said before I powered off the phone and dropped it into my purse.

I sang a song with Mont's name as he continued to dip in and out of my goodies. "I don't want to hear it," he said, as he slammed his blessing deep down into my soul. I cried out in sweet ecstasy as we both climaxed at the same time and fell flat on the bed. "Damn!" He cursed as he looked at me. "I just can't get enough of you. I'm not going to stop until you're all mine," he added, as I blinked slowly and fell asleep.

When my eyes fluttered, the entire room was dark. I jumped up and opened the black-out curtains to see that the sun was about to set.

"Mont, wake up. You've got to get me back to the coffee house and fast. It's after five in the evening. I can't believe that we slept so long,"

"That's what good loving will do to you. It'll put you to sleep," he joked as he yawned.

"You're absolutely correct. I'd love an instant replay of earlier, but I've got to pick up Tia and cook dinner," I replied, as he pulled me on top of him.

Even though I said we didn't have time to fool around again, we did. After another twenty minutes of Mont and his anaconda, I was hoarse and out of breath. I couldn't wait to go home and soak in a hot bath. I carefully checked my nude body for any marks before I wiped off at the sink. After cleaning myself up, Mont and I shared a long kiss before we stepped out into the hallway. As we were leaving the room, another couple passed by us and it looked like they were sneaking around too. I silently giggled to myself, as the woman stood behind the short, bald guy while he swiped the card through the slot in the door.

When we walked out of the hotel, I wasn't afraid that someone would see me anymore because the sun had set. I playfully jumped onto Mont's back for a few seconds before we reached the car. He carried me as I held on and planted the sweetest kisses on the side of his face. We both laughed as he carefully put me down on the passenger side of his car. After he unlocked the car, he opened the door for me. As I watched him walk around to the driver side of the car, I realized how much I still loved this man.

On the way back to the coffee house, he held my hand again. I felt so good, and I'd wished that I'd never married Trent at all. As we rode in silence, my body shuttered one last time from the mind blowing orgasms that Mont had given me. After being with him today, I prayed silently that Trent wouldn't be interested in having sex tonight. When I saw the coffee house in the near distance, I powered my cell phone on and started responding to Latria's text messages. I was happy to see that Trent hadn't called back. Shit, he may have been with Diamond. For all I knew, he could've been with her when he called and checked up on me earlier.

With Mont back in the picture, I debated if I wanted to meet up with Jason when he came to Virginia next month. Considering that he was a newbie, I didn't know how he would react after we had sex. He may try to put me on blast and contact Trent on the low. I guess this was just a chance that I was going to have to take because I was definitely going to get to know Jason better. I knew that Mont loved me and that he would never contact Trent about our rendezvous.

When Mont zoomed into the parking lot at the coffee house, he pulled up right beside my car. After he told me how much he enjoyed spending time with me, he kissed me on the back of my hand and wished me a good night. I told him that I'd had a good time as well and reached over and gave him a hug; then I got out of his car. I felt his eyes watching my backside as I unlocked and opened my car door. When I sat down in the driver's seat, I turned the engine on and looked to my left. He was looking my way, and I blew a kiss at him before I backed up out of the parking space. While I waited to exit the parking lot, I called Latria and talked to her until I reached my mother-in-law's house.

I filled her in on today's event with Mont. She listened quietly until I told her about Mont entering me from the back while I was on the phone with Trent. "Oh no girl, I know you couldn't handle that big thing. I can't believe he did that," she shrieked. "I took it like a pro, but when I got off of the phone with Trent, it was a different story," I laughed, as I replied. Just as I wrapped up our conversation about Mont and the hotel, I pulled up to get Tia.

Instead of going inside, I called Trent's mother and asked her to bring Tia out to the car. I didn't feel like going in after getting my back blown out. When Tia got in the car, my mother-in-law bent down and buckled her into her car seat.

"Hi Mommy Lyric, I missed you today," she said, as she waved goodbye to her grandmother.

"I missed you too. What did you do today?" I said as we turned out of the driveway.

"We went to the grocery store, and I helped Grammy shell some peas," Tia responded.

"Shell peas," I said, as I remembered that I needed to go stop by the grocery store.

I promised Trent that I was going to make him some spaghetti, but I didn't have any sauce.

"Yes ma'am, it was hard too. I don't like shelling peas."

"Well, mommy Lyric is never going to make you shell peas, but we do have to stop by the grocery store," I told her, as we pulled up at the grocery store.

"Okay, Mommy Lyric," she said, as she looked up at the bright BI-LO sign.

After we got out of the car, I put Tia in a shopping cart and we made our way to the spaghetti sauce aisle. I put two glass jars of sauce and a box of noodles in the shopping cart, just to be on the safe side. As I made my way down the aisle, I couldn't help but hear a conversation going on the next aisle over. "Oh my goodness, Diamond Murphy, is that you?" A lady asked in a high pitched voice.

If I would've had ears like a dog, they would've been standing straight up in the air. *"Did she say, Diamond Murphy?"* I asked myself silently. As the two ladies carried on their conversation, I curiously walked to the next aisle. I pretended to look at the boxes of cake mix as I looked at the two ladies. The one on the left was definitely Diamond. I remembered how she looked on the picture I'd seen in Trent's phone. She had a nice shape, polished nails, and a ring on her right hand that resembled my wedding ring.

I didn't notice it at first, but I'd pushed my shopping cart closer than I intended to. I was about five feet away from her when I decided that I was too close for comfort. I knew that Diamond didn't notice me because she was too busy yapping with her long-lost gal pal at the end of the aisle. As I pushed the shopping cart back to the spaghetti sauce aisle, I heard a phone ring from the next aisle over. "Give me just a second, I've got to answer this," said Diamond, while she put the conversation with her gal pal on hold. "Hello. No, I don't think you left it in my car. What phone are you calling me from now? The one in your office. Oh ok, well I'll check and see if your phone fell under the seat. Alright Tee," she said.

"Who the hell was Tee? Was that the nickname she had for Trent?" Just as the voice inside of my head instructed me to snatch the phone out of

Diamond's hand, Tia looked up and said, "Mommy Lyric, I have to go to the bathroom." I was so into Diamond that I'd forgotten Tia was with me, she had been so quiet. Considering that the restrooms were in the opposite direction, I didn't go back to the aisle that Diamond and her friend were on. I took Tia to the bathroom and when we came out, I headed right back to the aisle that the baking goods were on.

It looked as though I was a little too late to confront Diamond. She was already gone; I didn't even see the lady that she'd been talking to. After I picked up the link sausage and some prepackaged mushrooms, I checked out and left the grocery store. I looked around in the parking lot for Diamond, but I didn't know what kind of car she drove. That's the one piece of information that Latria didn't give to me.

I knew that I had to get home, but something inside of me wanted to drive by the funeral home where Trent worked. On my way there, I thought about calling Latria to ask her what kind of car Diamond drove, but I remembered that Tia was in the car, so I quickly messaged Latria while I was at the red light. I never got a response, so I drove to the funeral home and took a mental picture of every car that was parked in the spaces in front of the building.

I noticed that the lights in the foyer of the funeral home were on, as well as Trent's office light. There were only two cars in the parking lot and one of them belonged to Trent. The other was a gold sports car, and it looked like a BMW, but I wasn't sure because it was parked close to a bush. "Is that Daddy's job?" Tia questioned, as I was trying to remember the cars that were in the parking lot. "No baby that was another building that looks like your Daddy's job," I lied, as I took one final look and headed home to make Trent's spaghetti.

7

Fooling Around

My cell phone rang as the spaghetti sauce and fresh vegetables simmered on the stove top. After looking at the screen, I saw that Latria was calling and shooed Tia out the kitchen. Lord knows, I didn't want her telling Trent any of my secrets.

"Sorry Lyric, I was in the bath when you messaged me," she said.

"Girl, you wouldn't believe what happened. I ran into Diamond at the grocery store. I got close enough to her to see that she has a ring that resembles mine. I also overheard her cell phone conversation about a missing cell phone in her car. I'm not sure if it was Trent, but I think it was because she said the name Tee," I whispered, all in one breath.

"What? Who do you think Tee is, Trent?" She asked.

"Yes, that's why I wanted to know what kind of car she had. I overheard Diamond say that she was going to stop by Tee's office after she left the grocery store."

"Ok, I have the paper right here in front of me. It looks like Diamond has two cars. She has a white 2007 Infinity and a 2010 gold BMW coupe," she reported.

"A gold BMW coupe! I saw one of those in the parking lot at the funeral home tonight," I hissed, as I sat down in a chair at the table.

"Well, you know what that means," Latria said as we both sang in unison, "Trent's Tee."

"I can't believe this bullshit. I'm in here cooking for his no good behind, and he's probably kissing that heffa good night right now. What am I going to do?"

"First of all, calm down and keep your cool. Whenever Mr. Tee gets home act the same, you don't want him to have a clue that you know about his precious Diamond."

"Right," I added, as she continued her lecture.

"Have his dinner ready, bath water ran, and make sure you sex him good tonight too. After he falls asleep, get his phone again and see what the two of them have been up to."

"Alright, being nice to Trent tonight is going to be hard to do. I should spit in his food or something. Plus, I'm sore from being with Mont today."

"If spitting in his spaghetti makes you feel better, do it, and you should've known to save some loving for your husband," she said with a giggle.

After the both of us stopped laughing, I got serious and said, "Do you think that Trent has anymore female friends that I don't know about?"

"There's only one way for us to find out. You already know you need to go through his phone again. I'm sure if you keep looking you'll find more stuff. I think all men are dogs and that none of them are faithful," she answered.

Just then I saw a set of headlights flash across the window.

"I've got to go. I think that Mr. Tee just pulled in the driveway. I'll call or text you first thing in the morning," I said before I got off of the phone.

"Daddy," I heard Tia yell as the entry door opened. Even though I wasn't in the living room, I already knew that she had jumped into Trent's arms. When I walked around the corner, I saw the two of them hugging and he gave her a kiss on the cheek.

"It sure smells good in here. I can't wait to eat, but I should shower first. I smell like embalming fluid. Can you believe we got in three bodies today from the same nursing home?" He said as he took his shoes off.

I wanted to add a fourth body to the count and slap Trent upside the head with a skillet, but I hid my evil thoughts with a smile. After I kissed him on the cheek, I thought I smelled perfume.

"Yes, I can believe that. Do you want me to start the shower baby?"

"Nah, I'll start it myself," he answered, as he headed towards our bedroom.

I don't know what made me lie so fast, but I blurted out, "I tried to call you earlier, but you didn't answer."

"I'm sorry I misplaced my phone, I have it now, though. It was underneath the seat in the car."

At that very moment, I knew that Trent was Mr. Tee for sure.

Trent didn't shower long and joined me in the kitchen wearing a V-neck t-shirt and black thin pajama pants. It looked like he didn't have on any boxers at all. His blessing was hanging low, and I wondered if he was trying to seduce me as he leaned in and kissed me on the lips. I was mad as hell at him, but I couldn't resist his juicy lips and the smell of his Old Spice body wash. So, I kissed him back. As I turned around to see where Tia was, he rubbed his mini elephant trunk against my behind.

"Stop it, you know Tia's in the living room," I whispered, as he came closer.

"Like you said, she's in the living room," he whispered back, as he pinned me up against the counter and slipped his tongue across my lips.

Just as I felt the hardness of his erection, I heard Tia's footsteps coming in the direction of the kitchen. He backed off just in time, but his erection was evident in his thin pajamas. When he saw Tia's little head, he scooted quickly out of the kitchen.

When he returned, his erection had subsided, and his robe was closed with the belt tied in a loose knot in the front.

"Would you like soda or tea to drink with your dinner?" I asked him.

"Umm, I think I'd like some sweet tea."

"Mommy Lyric, I want sweet tea too," Tia chimed in.

"Okay, but only a little because you had an accident last night."

"Yes ma'am," she replied, as she settled herself in the chair at the table.

After I poured the drinks and fixed our plates, we sat down to eat. Shortly after I took a few bites of food, I made sure that my phone was in my back pocket and excused myself from the table. I put my plate in the microwave, went to our bedroom, and looked for Trent's work clothes. I knew that he wasn't smart enough to cover his filthy tracks when I saw his pile of dirty clothes near the shower. When I bent down, I dug in his pockets to see if his cell phone was there. Bingo, it was, and the blue notification light was blinking. I quickly entered Anna's birthday, "7787" and the phone unlocked.

I then strolled through his call log and saw calls from Diamond and another number that didn't have a name saved with it. I wondered who else Trent could be talking to for eighteen minutes, and it looked as though he'd ended the call right before he walked through the door. I took pictures of the unsaved number in Trent's call log and skimmed through his messages. I wasn't surprised to see messages from Diamond, but when I came across a picture of a nice firm apple bottom in hot pink boy shorts, I hesitated. I wondered whose ass that could be because it sure wasn't mine. I didn't own any underwear like that. With my face screwed up, I took a look at the picture one last time before I snapped a picture of the image with my cell phone.

When I was finished looking for evidence in his phone, I picked up his work shirt and it smelled like perfume. There also looked to be a smudge of makeup on the shirt. I tossed the shirt back to the floor and started to walk back to the kitchen when the voice inside of my head said, *"Check his boxers."* I was obedient to the voice and bent down to check them out. Trent's navy blue boxers were damp, and there were white stains on the front of them. This was the confirmation that I needed, he was definitely cheating.

Before I left the bathroom, I took pictures of his nasty cum stained underwear and the make-up smudged shirt. Then I sent the pictures to my email with Jason's hidden picture. When I left the bathroom, I laughed inside of my head and thought that this must be payback from all the women's husbands that I'd slept with over the years. I couldn't lie; I was hurt, but I knew that I would be okay. I'd survived a broken heart before, and I knew that I could do it again and beat Trent at his own game in the process.

After finding cum soaked underwear, I knew that I was on my way to not giving a damn again. My bangles clinked as I walked back into the kitchen where Trent and Tia were still eating. I remained quiet as I took my plate out of the microwave and sat back down at the table.

"Are you okay baby?" Trent asked.

"Yeah, I'm fine. My stomach has been acting up today. I think I ate something that didn't agree with me," I responded, as I drank from my cup.

Considering that I'd left the table to snoop around in his belongings, Tia and Trent finished eating before I did. I sat at the table all alone and messed over my warm spaghetti. Meanwhile, Trent ran Tia a bath and got her ready for bed. While they sang songs like, *The Itsy Bitsy Spider* and *Old McDonald had a Farm*, I sent Jason a quick text that read, "Hi." He responded immediately, "I just found out that I'll be coming to Virginia in two weeks instead of three. I was about to text you, when I saw your greeting." I was elated, and I replied with the message, "That's great. I can't wait to see you."

In the midst of messing over my spaghetti and texting Jason, I received a text from Mont that read, "Being with you today was out of this world. I still haven't taken a shower because I don't want to wash your scent off of me." I responded, "I haven't showered either, I just ate dinner and yes today was amazing. I miss spending time with you." Mont replied back with, "When can I see you again? We don't have to have sex. I only want to hold you in my arms and smother you with kisses." I blushed as I messaged, "Soon, I promise."

Just as I sent Mont's last text message, I responded to Jason, "I'm going to call you tomorrow. Sweet dreams." When I heard Trent and Tia in her bedroom, I cleared the table and put the dishes in the dishwasher. I then joined them in her room as Trent read her a story. I lay down beside her, and she snuggled close to me. It made me wonder what she would do without me. I was her Mommy Lyric, and we had developed a special bond.

I remembered the first time I met her. She wanted to sit beside me at the restaurant, and she even wanted to go home with me. I knew that leaving Trent also meant that I would have to leave Tia too. That wouldn't only hurt her; it would hurt me as well. I had to make my mind up, and I needed to do it fast. I was extremely confused about confronting Trent or just sweeping this whole Diamond thing under the rug. I knew that I'd messed up with Trent before we got married and I almost lost him. Maybe I should allow him to cheat to get even with me. I know I sound crazy, but this may be able to work out after all.

After Tia was sound asleep, we left her and headed to our master suite. When I entered the dimly lit room, I started undressing. As I started to strip, my clothes dropped to the floor in a pile. When I remembered that my phone was in my pants pocket, I bent down, removed it, and put it on the counter. Trent watched me as I ran a bubble bath. When he realized that he'd left his clothes on the floor, he came into the bathroom with me. While he sorted his clothes to put them in the hamper, he realized how stiff his boxers were and suggested that he start a load of laundry.

"Alright, take my clothes too," I said, as I picked up my soiled clothes and handed them to him. "Sure thing," he replied, as he pulled his phone out of his pants pocket. When Trent left to start the load of laundry, I dimmed the bathroom lights and stepped into the hot water in the bathtub. After I sat down, I pressed the button to turn on the jets. As I leaned my back against the wall of the tub, I felt like I was in heaven. I thought about the fun I'd had with Mont today at the hotel. I wondered what he was doing at this very moment. Could he possibly be thinking about me?

A small smile raised from the corners of my mouth. But, it didn't last long because Trent broke the silence with a question that made my heart skip a beat. "Did you have fun today?" I didn't know how to answer his question. I wasn't sure if it was a trick question or not, so I pretended like I didn't hear him. While the warm water bubbled around in the tub, I thought about how I would respond.

When Trent cleared his throat and asked again, I looked his way and replied, "No, all I did was window shop and have a cup of coffee downtown."

"I'm talking about at the grocery store," he said; then added, "Tia said that you zoomed her around the store like a race car."

I exhaled and replied, "Yeah, I just wanted to show her how fun grocery shopping could be."

"Can you do me a favor?" He asked.

"Sure, whatever you want Trent."

"After you dry off, can you come to bed naked?"

"I can do that," I replied with a seductive smile.

After my heart rate decreased, I washed and dried off. Then I headed to bed just like Trent asked me to. The cool sheets welcomed my warm oiled body. When Trent turned over, I realized he was naked and that his erection had returned. "I love you Lyric, you do know that don't you?" He asked, as he pulled me into his arms and kissed me. "Yeah, baby. I know that. I love you too." I said. I waited for Trent to say something else but he didn't. I felt movement and watched his silhouette as he disappeared under the sheets and spread my legs apart. When his tongue plunged into my pleasure zone, I closed my eyes and relaxed.

I stopped thinking about Mont and Diamond, and focused on Trent's oral capabilities. I started to swivel my hips and tug at the sheets. As he slurped up my love juices, I moaned a little and pushed his face deeper into my love box. When he came up for air, I had already climaxed and wet the bed. I was weak and didn't think I had anything left to give, but I was wrong. Trent rolled me over on top of him, and slid his thickness inside of me with no problem. I was a little tender from today's escapade with Mont, but I didn't let that stop me.

I gave it to Trent like I didn't know that he was cheating. The sex was almost as good as the sex that we had on our wedding night in Hawaii. Thirty minutes later, he finally reached his sexual peak. I was overjoyed when I was able to rest. My legs ached from being on top of him for so long. It'd felt like I had been riding a horse. All I wanted to do was go to sleep, and that's exactly what I did as soon as I rolled over.

I'm not sure how long I was asleep before Trent woke me up. He was kissing and sucking on my neck. I was a little irritated, but I turned over and kissed him on his soft lips. As the lids of my eyes shut again, I sleepily wrapped one of my legs around him. The next thing I knew we were having sex again. Only this time, he was on top, huffing and puffing. He made me feel real good, but I was worn out and couldn't wait until he climaxed, so I could go back to sleep.

That morning I stretched as I turned over to see what time it was. I couldn't believe that Trent kept me up half the night. We rolled around on our king size bed like pigs did in the cool mud until the wee hours of the morning. My love box was beyond sore, and I was certain that I had more than a few hickeys on my neck and breasts. It looked as though I'd slept through Trent's alarm and he'd already left for work.

When I sat up on the bed and yawned, I noticed a handwritten note, on my nightstand. After picking up the note, I saw two one hundred dollar bills underneath it. The note read:

Mrs. Morrison,

I took Tia to my mother's house. Take this money and buy yourself something nice. I love you, I'll call you later.

Love,
Mr. Morrison

That was so sweet, but I didn't feel like going anywhere. All I wanted to do was take a shower, eat breakfast, and wait for Latria to call me on her morning break. I couldn't wait to tell her about the evidence in Trent's phone and the wild sex from last night.

When my feet hit the floor, I reached for my phone on the nightstand. After I got my hands on it, I entered my code and walked to the bathroom. I started the shower and sat down on the toilet to urinate. While I sat there, I read text messages from Jason. I wonder if it was a good time to call him, it was a little after eleven here in Virginia, so that meant it was only five or six in the morning where he was. When the thought of being considerate crossed my mind, I decided to call Jason after my shower.

That would give him another twenty minutes or so to sleep. It's not like he needed his beauty rest because he was already too handsome for words. In the shower, I let the water rain down on top of my scalp. After I washed my hair, I shaved my legs and armpits. I accidentally nicked myself with the razor and blood poured from my knee cap. All this time I've been shaving, and I'd never cut myself until today. The cut wasn't deep, but it did sting.

When I turned the shower off, I heard my cell phone ringing. I quickly opened the shower door and wiped my feet on the mat only to slip as soon as I took a step onto the tile. I ended up falling flat on my behind and missed the phone call. Instead of getting up right away, I sat there and laughed at myself. I was thankful that I wasn't seriously injured, but I knew that I was going to be sore later.

Since I was afraid to stand up, I crawled over to the bath mat in front of the bathroom vanity and pulled myself up. I noticed the hickeys on the side of my neck as soon as I stood up. There were so many that it looked like someone tried to choke me. If I went out today, I was going to make sure I covered up these love marks with makeup. If I didn't, someone would surely think that I was being abused. After I dried off, I spread my towel on the floor and made sure there was no water on the tile.

Before I walked out of the bathroom, I grabbed my cell phone off of the granite counter. After entering my security code, I saw that I missed a call from Jason. I wondered what he was doing up this early as I called him back. While his phone rang, I walked by the mirror attached to our dresser and glimpsed an image of my naked body. I saw a greenish bruise starting to form on my buttocks, I knew that this was going to be an ugly bruise.

Just as I flopped down on the bed, Jason answered on his end, "Good morning," he said as he yawned. "Good morning," I replied back, as we started a conversation. We talked about any and everything. He talked mostly about his family that he was coming to visit here in

Virginia. They'd won big in the lottery and built a huge mansion out in the country. I didn't understand why someone would want to live in Virginia over Hawaii, but when Jason mentioned the active volcanoes I understood.

After talking about his rich, spoiled cousins, he asked about my marriage. I was a little hesitant to tell him at first, but I told him that I'd only been married for a couple of weeks and that things were going okay. That's when Jason told me something that confirmed Trent was no good.

"I saw you and your husband as soon as the two of you walked into the restaurant. You probably didn't notice me talking to the hostess, but I agreed to pay her twenty dollars if she sat you in my section so that I could meet you."

I interrupted and squealed, "Are you serious? I didn't even notice."

As he continued, he said, "Yeah, I'm dead serious. I figured that was the only way that I would get a chance to meet you because I wasn't sure if the man you were with was your brother, cousin, friend, or lover at the time. Anyway, before I came to your table, I saw your husband in the bathroom. He was on the phone with someone named Diamond. Even though he was in a corner, I could still hear bits of his conversation. I heard him say *"No, this isn't going to change anything between us and I'll be back in a few more days,"* As I washed and dried my hands, I tried to ignore him but I couldn't. He looked to be up to no good in that corner, and I wanted to give you a heads up. That fool might be trying to play you."

"Jason, I believe you. Thanks for sharing that information with me. I truly appreciate it," I replied.

"I wanted to tell you earlier, but all we've been able to do is text, and I didn't want to tell you news like that through a text message," he added in a somber tone.

"I'll be okay. I'm a big girl," I confirmed, as I changed the subject and told Jason about my minor injury with the razor and the fall in the bathroom this morning.

"Are you alright? If I were there I would kiss your boo-boo's and make them feel better," he said.

While Jason continued to talk, I wished more and more that he was here in Virginia.

8

Uninvited

After Jason and I got off of the phone, I slipped on some clothes and straightened up the house. While I vacuumed and dusted, I thought about the conversation that Jason and I had, and it hadn't shocked me at all. Trent and this Diamond lady must've had something going on before we got married. If that was the case, why didn't he marry her instead of me? Maybe she was an old heartthrob that he couldn't get over. Hell, for all I know she could have been the female version of Mont. Whatever the reason or connection I wanted to know if he loved her at one point in time or if he was in love with her. I didn't think I could take any more of this, and deep down I was ready to confront Trent.

When the thought of calling Latria crossed my mind, I didn't follow through. I ended up sending her a text message and asked her if she could come to my house after she got off work. While I waited for her response, I filled a bowl with Lucky Charms and turned the television on in the living room. After I had eaten the cereal, I lay on the couch and watched reruns of *Martin*. That Sheneneh was really something else.

Two hours and four episodes later, my cell phone rang. It was Latria; she confirmed that she was off work and on the way to my house.

I yawned after we ended the short phone call and stood up to stretch. I knew that Latria was going to be hungry when she got here, so I decided to prepare a few appetizers. After I took a bag of frozen hot wings out of the freezer, I looked in the cabinet to see if there was a bag of chips and can of chili. Luckily there were a few cans, so I made some chili cheese dip to go with the hot wings. When the appetizers were in the oven and the timer was turned on, I took two wine glasses down from the cabinet.

While I waited for Latria to ring the doorbell. I started watching another episode of *Martin* and sent Mont a text message, but I didn't get a response. I wondered what he was doing and secretly craved some of his mother's sweet potato casserole. During a commercial break, I looked in the refrigerator and tried to decide which bottle of wine Latria and I were going to drink. Then the doorbell chimed and the timer went off on the stove, and I was torn between unlocking the door and taking the food out of the oven.

I figured that I'd better let Latria in first, because I didn't want her to cuss me out for leaving her outside for too long. After I closed the door on the refrigerator, I shouted, "I'm coming Latria." I walked quickly but cautiously in my socks across the hardwood floors because I didn't want to slip and fall again. I already had a bruised rear end that was probably black and blue by now. When I reached the entry door, I didn't look to see who it was; I assumed it was Latria because she was the only person I had been expecting.

After I unlocked the entry door, I flung it open and headed back to the timer going off in the kitchen. "Latria, come on in here girl. I got something to tell you and before you say anything about the marks on my neck, they're hickeys- not an act of criminal domestic violence," I confirmed, as I pulled the dip and the hot wings out of the oven. Just as I sat the baking dish and the tray of wings on a cooling rack, I heard her enter the kitchen. "Why are you so quiet today? Did someone piss you off at the DMV?" I asked as I turned around. To my surprise, Mont was standing there.

"Mont, what the hell are you doing here?" I screamed as I ran back to the entry door to look outside.

"My car isn't out there if that's what you're looking for. I had my new driver drop me off," he said, as he pulled a chair out from under the table and made himself at home.

"You can't be here, this is unacceptable, and you know it," I sputtered as I walked back to the kitchen.

"Admit it. You're happy to see me. I know that you were thinking about me because you just sent me a text message, not even thirty minutes ago," he smoothly said.

"Yeah, but that doesn't give you the right to come here to my house. What if Trent were home?"

"Oh, I knew he wasn't here because his car was parked in Diamond's driveway," he boldly stated.

"What?" I stuttered as I sat down.

"Lyric, I'm sorry to tell you this, but Trent's no good for you," he said, as he slid his phone over and pointed at the screen.

I grabbed the phone and looked at the image. It was a picture of Trent's car parked in someone's driveway. I wasn't sure if it was Diamond's house, but the house number 1013 was in the image, so I would definitely ask Latria about this when she got here. After I slid Mont's phone back to him, I put my head down on the table. "I know he's cheating already," I confided in a muffled voice as I talked to Mont with my head buried in my arms. I wanted to cry, but I couldn't bring myself to coming undone in front of him.

Even though I'd cried in front of him a million times before, this time was different. I knew this was exactly what he'd hoped for. The fact of the matter was that he didn't want Trent to have me because he wanted me all to himself. With my head down, I thought of Mont's message he'd left me on the night of my honeymoon. He said that he'd be waiting for me with open arms. I immediately wondered if Mont knew something about Trent before we'd gotten married. If he did, I wondered why he didn't tell me. He could've saved me from this heartbreak. Maybe I was jumping the gun, but it seemed that Mont had a little private eye in him. I don't know why it took me so long to notice, I wouldn't be surprised if he knew about Jason.

Just as I felt that my head was about to explode, I heard movement that brought me back to reality. I couldn't see what Mont was doing with my head down, but I had a feeling he was moving in to console me. Before he could even make it to the other side of the table, I lifted my head up and said, "I think you should go." As tears welled up in my eyes, he agreed with me and bent down to kiss me on the top of my head. I really wanted to ask him for a hug, but I knew better than that. If he got any closer to me, I knew that my panties would end up on the floor.

As soon as Mont called his driver back he left, not to long after that Latria came. When she walked in she had a bottle of wine, which was a good thing because I had drank an entire bottle of Moscato and was working on another. After she sat down at the kitchen table, I told her about Mont's visit and her mouth hit the floor.

"So you're telling me that Mont just left this house not too long ago?"

"Yes, and he had a picture of Trent's car parked in Diamond's driveway," I replied.

"Girl, get the hell out of here. Wait a minute. I know that you told Mont about Trent's cheating, but you didn't tell him Diamond's name when you guys were at the hotel the other day did you?" She asked with wide eyes.

"Nope, I sure didn't. I don't know how he knows everybody's business."

"What was the house number where Trent's car was parked?" She asked.

"1013, it was a brick house with white shutters. His car was parked in front of a closed garage door. Her cars must've been inside of the garage because I didn't see them," I reported.

As Latria dug inside of her purse, I got up and fixed each of us each a plate of dip and wings. When I got the sour cream and ranch dressing out of the refrigerator, she said, "1013 Butler Lane, yep. That's the slut bucket's address." After Latria confirmed the truth of Mont's picture with the crumpled information from the DMV, I poured myself another drink.

For the remainder of the evening, we sat at the table and gossiped. I put Trent and his cheating in the back of my mind and enjoyed my friend. I laughed so hard at Latria that my side ached. When she suggested that she leave, I realized that Trent and Tia would be home soon, and I didn't have a clue about what to make them for dinner. "I need to go to the grocery store, but I think that I'm too buzzed to drive. Can you take me?" I asked.

"Yeah, I need to go to the store too. Get your shoes, I'll be waiting for you in the car.

After I put my shoes on, I joined her in her car. When I sat down in the warm leather seat, I smiled. Latria had turned on the seat warmer. She knew that I was cold blooded.

"So what grocery store do you want to go to?" She asked me as I strolled through my text messages.

"The one that's closest to 1013 Butler Lane." I answered with an evil grin.

"Oh, I see what type of party this is," she said as she pulled over to the side of the street, and entered the address into the GPS in her car.

While the system calculated the route and distance to Diamond's house, we waited in silence. When the system was all done, Latria made an illegal U-turn in the middle of the street. We passed by three grocery stores on the way to Diamond's house. I made a mental grocery list in my head as we passed by brick house after brick house. They all looked alike to me, but when I saw the brick house with the numbers 1013 on the front of it, I sat up straight and peered out the tinted window. I guess she didn't care about having a high light bill because it looked as though every light in the house was on.

As we slowly passed by, I saw movement in the garage. Little Miss. Diamond was doing something in there. I wondered what she was up to, as we left the neighborhood and headed to the grocery store.

"Did you see anything?" Latria asked.

"Yeah, I saw her. She was in the garage. I'm not sure what she was doing though. You didn't see her?" I asked with irritation in my voice.

"I sure didn't, I was driving. I got a glimpse of the cars in the driveway, but that was it."

"Damn, she was right there. You should've looked. I wanted you to see her," I bickered.

"How in the hell am I going to look and drive? Did you want me to crash into someone's parked car or mailbox? You know that I've been drinking too," she cursed.

"My bad, you're right. The last thing that we need to do is get in an accident. That definitely wouldn't look good considering that you work at the DMV and all," I laughed.

An entire week had passed before I knew it. Things were normal around the house because I hadn't confronted Trent. He'd still been taking Tia to his mother's house every day, so I had a lot of time to myself. I was really enjoying relaxing around the house without having Tia on my heels. I loved her, but she could be a bit demanding with her sandwich bags full of cereal and countless Disney movies. Having to entertain a toddler drained me, deep down I was happy that Trent took advantage of his mother living so close.

Speaking of Trent, he couldn't keep his hands off of me lately. As he walked by me, he'd reach out and squeeze one of my breasts or smack me on my butt. I knew I was a good catch, but my goodness, his displays of affection were starting to feel like I was being groped. He and I had only had sex one time in the past week, he wanted it more, but I turned him down. I even pretended that I was asleep, and he rubbed his penis against my behind one night. Don't get me wrong, I was still attracted to him, but the thought of him being with someone else sexually made me feel sick. I know that's strange for me, but if he was spending time with Diamond, at least three times a week, why in the hell did he still want my sex.

Other than the fact that I was his wife and that he had a high sex drive was the only two reasons that I could think of. The truth was that I hadn't been feeling very sexual over the past week. I missed Mont, and I thought about him often. But, I didn't dare text or call him because I feared that he would show up at my house again. What he did last week really scared the shit out of me. If Trent caught Mont in our house, he'd kill me and then the two of them would probably end up killing each other. I didn't even want to imagine anything like that happening because Mont was never going to step foot across our threshold again, and I was going to make sure of that.

On a positive note, the bruise on my butt from my slip and fall had vanished along with the love marks that Trent left on my neck. With only a few more days until Jason touched down, I was ecstatic. We'd been talking more and more over the past week, and I wondered if we would still contact one another after we hooked up. There was power in sex; it was crazy how sex could make or break a relationship. I didn't know how sex could change people until I thought back to the time I had sex with Latria's cousin. That Vienna sausage penis definitely made me have a change of heart.

Checking Trent's phone in the middle of the night was getting boring to me. So, I stopped the day after Mont came over uninvited. I already knew that I was going to find exactly what I was looking for. There were messages and calls from Diamond and that other unsaved number. Latria and I couldn't figure out who the number belonged to, though. It's too bad she didn't work for the phone company instead of the DMV. We even called the number, but no one answered, and the voicemail wasn't set up. Mont had been texting me on a regular, but I didn't respond to any of his messages.

I often think of the time that Mont proposed to me in my old apartment. That ring was pure perfection. Even though Trent had my hand in marriage, Mont still had my heart, and I think he knew that. I was torn between leaving and staying. Just like the song, *Get it Together* by that 90's girl group 702. I knew that if I saw him again, I probably wouldn't be able to stop myself from confessing my undying love for him. That's why I had to avoid Mont.

Today was the day. I'd just received the text that Jason's flight landed here in Virginia. I had butterflies in the pit of my stomach all morning, and I even woke up before Trent did. When his alarm went off, I pretended to be asleep. For the past couple of weeks Trent had been taking Tia to his mom's house, but today he didn't. He left her asleep in the bed with me. After he left, I showered and lounged around until Jason called me. As soon as I saw the number pop up on the screen of my phone, I got Tia dressed and dropped her off at her Grammy's. Luckily, the hotel that Jason was staying at was next to a Target, so I left my car there and walked to the hotel. Before I went into the lobby, I put a pair of shades and an old Atlanta Braves hat. After rereading the last text message that he sent, I got on the elevator and pressed the number 3.

Jason was on the third floor in the room at the end of the hallway. I knocked on the door when I approached room 308. The door opened a tiny bit, and I saw those gorgeous eyes of his. I didn't know who was smiling harder him or me. As soon as I walked into the room, he shut the door and locked it. We shared a hug and sat down at the small table in the room.

"Wow, I can't believe that you're here," Jason said.

"Me either," I replied as I blushed.

"It's really good to see you. I've been looking at the pictures that you sent every single day," he admitted.

"Well, I'm here now, so let's get to know each other a little better," I suggested as I got up out of the chair and sat down on Jason's lap.

From there the day only got better. We didn't have sex, we only ordered a large cheese pizza with pineapples and lay across the bed. We talked and talked until it was time for him to go out with his rich cousins. I was going to leave, but he insisted that I stay until he showered and got dressed. I even helped him decide on which outfit he should wear. Before I left, I kissed him quickly on the lips and got out of there because his cologne was making me horny. I wanted him, but I didn't push it. I knew that it would happen soon.

The very first day with Jason was a breath of fresh air. Of course, I told Latria about everything and she couldn't believe that Jason and I didn't have sex. We talked for the entire ride home, and I ended the call when I pulled up in my driveway. When I saw that Trent was home from work already, I wondered why he didn't call me and tell me, he usually did. Maybe he and Diamond got into it or something, and he decided not to go over to her house today. Whatever the reason, I gave myself a look over in the rear view mirror and went inside the house.

It smelled like Trent was inside cooking fish. I liked to eat fish, but I didn't like the smell that it left in your house after you were done frying it. I had to make sure that whatever I wore to see Jason in tomorrow was extra fresh, I didn't want to smell like fish. That would be an automatic turn off.

Before I made my way into the house, I kicked my shoes off. "Hey, guys. I'm home," I announced as I entered the kitchen. After my announcement Trent said, "Hey baby," as he looked up from the fish he was frying. I moved in quickly and planted a kiss on his cheek; then I went to check on Tia in her bedroom. She was only playing with her dolls, so I sat down and played with her until Trent called for us to eat.

I cautiously removed the bones from Tia's fish before I handed her plate to her. Then I begin to eat too, the fish dinner hit the spot. We talked for a while, and Tia told us about her Christmas list that she left at her Grammy's house. That child wanted some of everything. Teddy bears, coloring books and more baby dolls. Her room was full of half-naked doll babies, I didn't know what she was going to do with more of them. But, whatever she wanted I planned on getting it for her.

After the kitchen was clean, I raised the small window over the sink to let out the fishy odor that lingered in the air. While Trent took out the Trash and got Tia ready for bed, I stripped, took a shower, and washed my hair. I was exhausted but excited; I hoped that the night would quickly pass so that I could see Jason in the morning.

The next morning, I woke up a few minutes before Trent's alarm clock sounded. I lay in bed with my eyes open and looked around the room. I thought about what I would wear today until the alarm sounded and I closed my eyes. When Trent rolled over, he hesitated before he got out of bed. I wanted to roll over into his warm spot, but I resisted the urge and stayed put on my side of the bed. After he shut the alarm off, he went into the bathroom and closed the door. I opened my eyes and tried to hear what he was doing. It was very quiet, and I assumed that Trent was on the toilet.

After laying perfectly still with my eyes open, I heard Trent's voice in the bathroom. He was talking to someone in a baritone whisper. I wanted to get up and listen at the door, but I couldn't risk getting caught. Plus, I didn't want Tia to know that I was awake yet because she would want to stay with me today and that would throw a monkey wrench in the plans that I had with Jason. As much as it killed me, I stayed put in bed. When I heard little footsteps coming closer to my bedroom door, I closed my eyes again. I knew it was Tia.

I heard her as she pushed our bedroom door open. "Daddy, I want cereal," she said as she climbed on our king size bed. Trent didn't respond from the bathroom. I guess he didn't hear her because he was too busy whispering on the phone. After Tia settled on Trent's side of the bed, she yelled, "Daddy, I'm hungry." That's when I heard the bathroom door open, and Trent say, "Shh, don't wake up mommy. I'll be out in just a second." "Okay daddy," Tia replied.

As soon as he closed the bathroom door, I felt her inch closer to me. I didn't know what she was about to do to me, but I knew that she was about to do something. While I tried my best to keep my eyes shut, Tia took her little finger and attempted to pry one of my eyelids open. "Mommy Lyric, I want to stay with you today," she said in a whisper. My eyeball rolled around from side to side as she continued to flip my eyelid open and closed. When I didn't open my eyes, she gave up and climbed over my body. After I heard her feet hit the floor, and the television come on in the living room, I opened my eyes.

I rubbed the eye that Tia had been playing with, only to close my eyes quickly again because Trent came out of the bathroom. I turned over so he couldn't see my face and listened to his movement. When I heard him and Tia talking, I knew that he was in the living room. By this time, I wanted to check my phone, so I took a chance and grabbed it off the nightstand. Before I had a chance to look at the screen, I heard Trent on his way back into our bedroom.

I quickly shoved the phone underneath the covers and waited for Trent to get dressed and leave. Before he left, he bent down and kissed me on the cheek. Not much longer after that, I heard him tell Tia to grab her things. Then the entry door closed and there was complete silence. When I heard the car engine turn on, I got up and peeked out of the window. Trent and Tia were in the car and buckled up. I was going to lay back down, but I knew they were going to leave soon, so I got up and started the shower. The house still had a faint fishy odor, and I wasn't about to go anywhere smelling like fish.

The shower not only left me feeling refreshed but a little brand new. I washed my hair again too, just to be on the safe side. After dressing in a pair of stretch pants and a tight long sleeve top, I shut the window over the sink in the kitchen and set the alarm. Before I pulled out of the driveway, I called Jason, and he was already up. After requesting breakfast from Hardee's, I agreed to bring him whatever his heart desired.

The line at the restaurant was very long. I saw it before I pulled into the parking lot. I knew that Hardee's had great breakfast, but this was ridiculous. I started to go inside and order our food, but I changed my mind fast when I saw Tia and my mother-in-law getting out of her car. I watched them both as they walked hand in hand across the parking lot. Tia skipped a little as she held on tight to her doll baby with her free arm. Before they walked by my car, I turned the radio down and slid down in the seat.

I prayed that they didn't see me as the car in front of me moved forward. It was a good thing that my windows were tinted, or they would have definitely noticed me. When it was my turn to order, I only rolled the window down halfway, after I placed my order I rolled the window back up and waited impatiently for the line to move forward. At the window, I paid for the food and didn't even check my bag to see if the lady at the window had given me the correct order.

9

Coming Undone

When I pulled into the Hotel parking lot, I drove around to the back and parked near some overgrown bushes. After I shoved the bag of food down into the small bag that I'd packed, I called Jason to let him know that I was downstairs. When he didn't answer the phone, I immediately called back. I wondered where he was because he knew that I was coming. I'd only talked to him twenty minutes ago. After debating on going to his room or waiting in the car to see if he would call back, I decided to go inside and knock on the room door.

Whenever I got out the car, I walked around the building and went straight through the lobby. I didn't make eye contact with anybody. I boarded the elevator with one of the workers. I started to tell her good morning, but she looked irritated so I didn't. She probably didn't want to be here. Unlike me, she didn't have a strapping young man waiting for her in a room upstairs. When the elevator stopped the ill worker got off, and the doors of the elevator closed.

Next was my stop. Just as I thought of calling Jason again, my cell phone rang. It was him, and he apologized that he'd missed my call. He said that he was in the shower as I walked closer to his room door and knocked on it. "Hold on someone is at the door," he said. "I know, it's me silly," I laughed as I replied. "Oh," he said before hanging up the phone and opening the door.

I knew that he'd just gotten out of the shower but my God, I wasn't ready to see him like this. He was only wearing a towel wrapped around his waist and a pair of Jordan slides. He kissed me on my cheek and took my bag as soon as I walked through the door. My eyes followed his damp body as he put my bag on the foot of the bed. His hair was down his back, and it was just as wavy and curly as mine was. As much as I tried to I couldn't resist, lust had a hold of me.

I pushed him down on the bed; he looked surprised as I took my shirt off and straddled him. I ran my fingers through his wet hair, looked into his gorgeous eyes and said, "I hope I'm not coming on too strong." "Nah, you're good," he replied with a small smile that revealed his dimples. Then our lips met, and our tongues got familiar with one another. His hands caressed my hips and behind as I started to move slowly on top of him.

When his towel came undone, I reached down and massaged his man meat. Just as the tip got slippery, I slid down face to face with it and took him into my mouth. That's when I realized that Jason wasn't in the same category as Trent and Mont when it came to length and size. But that was okay because he looked to be about 8 inches or so in length, and I could definitely work with that. Jason placed his hands on the back of my head as I pleased him. He moaned and begged me to stop as my head bobbed up and down before he climaxed.

I did as I was told, and he rolled on top of me and pulled my pants off. Needless to say, he returned the favor and then slid on a condom before he entered me. He was finally inside of me, just knowing that we were connected did something to me. "Let me get on top," I demanded as we switched positions. With me on top now, I rode him at a slow and steady pace. I bent down and planted the sweetest, sexiest, kisses on his lips. As I neared my sexual peak, I sucked on his bottom lip and kissed him on his neck. Even though Jason wasn't packing like Mont or Trent, he surprised me. Being with him was a very pleasurable experience.

For the remainder of that day we lay in bed naked. I think that we kissed over a thousand times. I hated to leave him and even daydreamed about spending the night. Before I left that day we had sex again, this time, the sex was rough. The sex was so rough that the condom broke, not once but twice. I was a little worried about the condoms breaking, especially after Jason talked about how warm and wet my love box felt. I wondered if the condom broke at the beginning of our sex act or if it broke when we were near the end and he didn't withdraw himself. Whatever the case, he put on another condom and finished the job before we shared a shower, and I left.

Over the next two days, I was on cloud nine. I couldn't wait to wake up and drive to Jason's hotel. I felt like a school girl all over again. When I was with him, thoughts of Trent's cheating were far from my mind. Being with Jason had made my week, and I was so glad that he came to visit early. After hanging out with him at the Hotel room for those days made me feel like I'd known him my entire life. It was something about him that made me want more of him and I planned on meeting up with him again when he came back to Virginia to visit.

On the same day that Jason was set to leave, I got a bit emotional. We lay wrapped up in each other's arms for almost an hour before he left. I offered to take him to the airport, but he didn't think it would be a good idea. I lay there with my nose up to his neck and snorted his scent into my nostrils like it was a drug. He smelled so good; I didn't want him to leave. He promised that he would send a text message as soon as he landed back in Hawaii. Then we shared a slow sensual kiss at the door before we said our final goodbye.

Immediately after I left the hotel, I called Trent and asked him to bring some Chinese food home because I didn't feel like cooking. He agreed and hurried off the phone before I could ask him if he wanted me to pick Tia up, so I didn't bother. I passed right by his mother's house and didn't even slow down. I wondered if Trent was at Diamond's house, then all of a sudden I was on my way to 1013 Butler Lane. I wanted to see if his car was parked in her driveway and it was.

I thought about stopping and making a scene, but I didn't have the energy. I was drained, over the past few days, I'd given all of my attention and energy to Jason. Even though he was only here for five days, we had sex eight times. I shook my head as I thought about turning around and going back to Diamond's house. After I had made my mind up, I headed home, took a shower, and watched television in bed until I fell asleep.

When I woke up in the middle of the night, Trent was in bed sleeping beside me. I couldn't believe that I had been asleep that long. As I sat up in bed, I wondered if Jason made it home yet. With as little movement as possible, I reached for my cell phone to see if he had sent a text message and there wasn't one. *"He had to be back in Hawaii by now,"* I thought as I headed to the bathroom to urinate. While glimpsing in the direction of Trent's nightstand, he turned over and started to snore even louder. That's when a familiar blue light caught my eye.

Curiosity was getting the best of me when I did something that I hadn't done for a while. I tiptoed over to Trent's nightstand and took his phone into the bathroom. I sat on the edge of the bathtub as I entered his code. When I saw that he'd changed his screensaver from our wedding picture to a picture of Diamond, my blood began to boil.

I couldn't believe that he'd done that. As I continued to plunder through the text messages, I saw that he had been sending pictures of his blessing to several unsaved phone numbers. He wasn't the only one sending pictures. I expected to see images of Diamond, but there were so many pictures of breasts and rear ends that it looked like a porn website. The pictures weren't tasteful at all. These women had no shame in their game because their faces were in the pictures too.

The next thing I knew, my breathing changed, tears were falling, and I was on my way back into the bedroom.

"Trent, get your ass up," I yelled, as I flipped on the switch in the bedroom.

He jumped, as he sat up and rubbed his eyes.

"What happened, baby? Is something wrong?" He asked, with sincerity in his voice.

"What the hell is this shit? Who is Diamond and who are these naked women on your phone?" I cried, as I threw his phone beside him on the bed.

"How did you get on my phone? How did you know the code?" He said as he jumped up off of the bed and closed the room door.

"Really Trent? Is that all that you're concerned about? Using Anna's birthday wasn't as smart as you thought it was. I figured it out in no time, and I've been checking your phone for the past month. I've seen it all and I know that you've been going to 1013 Butler Lane too."

"Please stop yelling, you're going to wake Tia, and I don't want her to see us fighting," he said.

I could feel my forehead breaking out in a cold sweat.

"You need to explain this to me, and you need to explain it now," I commanded, as he sat on the bed and looked like a sad puppy.

"All I can tell you is I'm sorry. I'm not perfect Lyric, and you aren't either."

"That's all you've got to say?" I asked as I unlocked my cell phone and threw it at him. "Go ahead. Look through my phone, I guarantee you won't find any pictures of naked men or their penises," I shouted.

Luckily Trent didn't accept my offer and go through my phone because I hadn't deleted any messages from Mont or Jason. I didn't know what the hell was wrong with me. I almost ratted myself out. I guess my emotions had got the best of me.

"For goodness sake, settle down," Trent said as he stood up and walked towards me.

"What the hell do you mean settle down? We haven't even been married a month, and you're jeopardizing our marriage over some freak of the week," I said in a rage.

"Lyric, please baby just calm down, you're overreacting. It's only a few pictures," he replied as he dropped down to his knees in front of me.

"Okay, I'll calm down," I sarcastically said, while I looked under the bed and retrieved our brown leather luggage set. "I'll settle down, but it won't be here. I'm going home."

"Home?" Trent questioned and then added, "This is your home."

"I'm going to Stone Dale Court," I shouted while I madly snatched my belongings out the drawers and off the hangers in the closet.

After I grabbed my favorite pair of pajamas, I closed the biggest suitcase and zipped it shut. While Trent watched me, his mouth moved, but I didn't even hear what he was saying. He could have been apologizing or begging me not to leave. Hell, at this point I didn't care because I'd just collected my cosmetics and toiletries out of the bathroom and dumped them into my polka dot carry-on bag. After I grabbed my purse, I put the strap attached to the carry-on bag over my shoulder and rolled the suitcase to the entry door.

Trent stood in front of the door and whispered, "Lyric, please don't do this. We can work this out. Tia and I need you." "Get the hell out of my way," I demanded in a stern voice. I think I startled Trent because he jumped and moved out of the way. When I opened the door, I didn't look back as I rolled the suitcase off of the porch, down the steps, and onto the sidewalk. I put my things in the car quickly and burned rubber out of the driveway. As tears dripped off of my chin, I beat my fist on the steering wheel and wished that I would have punched Trent.

I called mom as soon as I got down the road, but her line was busy. I wanted her to know that I was on my way over. Maybe she'd left the phone off the hook by accident. Since I couldn't reach my mother, I called Latria, but she didn't pick up. The next person that came to mind was Jason. I called him, and he answered on the first ring. I talked to him until I reached my mother's house. To my surprise, the front door was open, and my mom was standing there in her robe. When I saw her with the cordless phone up to her ear, I knew that she was on the phone with Trent.

Before I could unbuckle my seat belt, she hung up the phone and shoved it into the pocket of her robe. When I stood up, I said, "What did Trent say to you?" After she shook her head, she replied, "He told me that you were on your way and that you were upset because of something you found on his cell phone." "That's 100% correct," I replied, while I gathered my things from the back seat. As I entered the entryway to the house, the familiar smell calmed my nerves. Mom then asked if I wanted some warm tea and I declined. After that, she embraced me with a hug, and we both went upstairs with my things.

When I woke up the next morning, I didn't know where I was. I sat up and looked around like I was crazy until I heard voices talking in the distance. After I realized that I was in my old room, I lay back down and pulled the covers over my head. *Did last night really happen?* I asked myself as I pulled the covers off of my head and saw my luggage near the foot of the bed. Yep, it happened. I felt horrible after I thought about how I carried on with Trent, knowing good and well that I was doing the very same thing that he had been doing.

I needed a cup of coffee, and I needed it now. I knew there was some brewing downstairs because I smelled it. Before I headed downstairs, I washed my face, but I didn't brush my teeth yet. Coffee tasted terrible if you drank it as soon as you brushed your teeth. Just thinking about the tart taste made me cringe.

Mom was making breakfast when I entered the kitchen. To my surprise, Boogie was in the kitchen too, he was sitting at the counter. It shocked me, and I wanted to run back upstairs to get dressed. Even though Boogie has seen me in my pajamas countless times when we were younger, it seemed different now. After we'd kiss the other day, I viewed him differently. "Good morning," Mom and Boogie said in unison as I sat on the barstool beside Boogie. Before I replied, I wished that I would have brushed my teeth. "Good morning," I said with a fake smile.

I knew that Boogie knew something was wrong. Why else would I be at my mother's house in my pajamas when my husband wasn't here. Since I'd already told Boogie about Trent's infidelity the other day, I went ahead and spilled the beans about what happened last night. Mom and Boogie listened inquisitively as they drank their coffee and ate their breakfast. I didn't have an appetite, so I drank my coffee in between telling them what happened.

After I told the entire side of my story, I heard my cell phone ringing from upstairs. I knew it was probably Trent, so I ignored it and continued listening to mom as she talked.

"After talking to Trent last night, I got the feeling that he was sincerely apologetic. I think you need to sit down and talk to him. The two of you have only been married a month and I'm sure you guys can work this out."

Then Boogie added his two cents.

"I don't know this dude, but he was dead wrong for having those pictures of those women on his phone. I know that's he regrets it because you're a great catch and from what your mom says his little girl absolutely adores you."

After taking a deep breath, I replied to the both of them by saying, "I'll think about talking to him but it won't be anytime soon. I don't want to see him at all. I may scratch his eyeballs out or knock him over the head with something."

Just as soon as I said that, the doorbell rang. I knew it was him, so I told mom to go to the door. While mom walked towards the front of the house, Boogie gave me a look. I shook my head and put my finger up to my lip, telling him to be quiet so I could hear.

We sat at the counter and turned our heads in the direction of the front hall. When mom opened the door, Trent greeted her, "Good morning, I'm sorry to stop by unexpectedly, but I tried calling Lyric, and she didn't answer. Can you get her for me?"

"I'm afraid not Trent, Lyric isn't ready to talk to you. Give her a few days and maybe she'll come around," Mom replied.

"Can you tell her that I'm sorry and tell her Tia asked about her this morning," Trent urged.

"Yeah, I'll let her know," mom replied in a hopeful tone.

Then we heard the entry door close.

As mom came around the corner, she said, "He looks a mess Lyric. He wants you back so bad. The poor thing."

"He'll be okay and mom you wouldn't be saying that if you actually saw the pictures and text messages that I copied off of his phone. You probably would have thrown the remainder of the grits on him, if you saw all of that nastiness." I flatly replied.

"You've got evidence?" Boogie chuckled with a smile and bright eyes.

"Yeah, I'll show you later because I know how nasty you are," I said with a laugh.

"Let me get out of here because I don't like the way this conversation is going," Mom announced, as she left the two of us sitting at the counter.

For the rest of the day, Boogie and I hung out. It felt like we were seventeen all over again. I was happy that we didn't cross the line because I couldn't risk messing our relationship up. After watching a few episodes of *Saved by the Bell,* we decided that we would visit Melody's grave. It didn't take me long to get dressed because I didn't have a huge selection of clothes to choose from. I was so upset last night that I didn't pay attention to what I'd been throwing in the suitcase.

I got dressed in a pair of Levi's and a pullover *PINK* sweater and we were ready to go. We were going to take my car, but Boogie insisted that we take his new snow white Dodge Challenger for a spin. After I told mom that we were leaving, we walked down the street to Boogie's mother's house. As we approached the driveway, I had a flashback of Boogie with his shirt off in the yard that day. I immediately blocked the image from my mind as I checked out Boogies new whip. It was real nice. I hoped I'd never have to ride in the back seat, because it was tiny.

After Boogie had shown me all the bells and whistles on his new car, we were ready to ride. We rode with the windows down and the music up. This car could really haul ass. I'd never rode in one of these, but I considered going to test drive a few. As the music blared, I thought about what happened last night and wondered if I would give Trent another chance. Deep down, I didn't know if I could. I would have to stay at mom's house until I made my mind up. I didn't know how long that would take, but I already missed Tia.

When we left the cemetery, I thought it would be a good idea to stop by my house and get a few more items while Trent wasn't home. After telling Boogie about my plans, he agreed to take me without any hesitance. After I gave him the turn-by-turn directions, he made a right turn onto our road, and our house was on the left. To my surprise, Trent was home, and he had company. I didn't want Boogie to know that the gold BMW that was parked in my driveway wasn't supposed to be there. "I'll be right back," I said as calmly as I could before I got out of the car.

My entire body shook as I made my way onto the porch. I didn't know what I was about to do, and I even debated about turning around for a millisecond. That's when the voice inside of my head told me to unlock the door. I did as the voice instructed, and I quietly took my keys out of the pocket of my hoodie and unlocked the entry door. As soon as I opened the door, I caught Trent and Diamond in mid- embrace. The looks on their faces were priceless as I walked in and said, "Don't mind me, I'm just here to get the rest of my shit."

"It's not what you think Lyric, let me explain," Trent replied as he stood up and started following me.

"Don't even think about touching me with those filthy hands of yours and don't waste your breath asking me to stay because I'm not," I yelled, as I tucked several flattened cardboard moving boxes under my armpit and stormed by Trent.

When I reached the living room, Diamond was digging into the cushions of the sofa. She looked frightened when I walked by her and flipped the couch over and yelled, "Whatever you're looking for, you better find it before I come back out of that bedroom." She didn't say anything, she only scrambled to the floor to her knees and grabbed her car keys.

As Diamond picked her designer purse up off of the floor, Trent rolled the sofa back to the correct position and stood in front of me while I snapped at Diamond.

"This is why I'm back to get the rest of my stuff, because of this slut right here," I shouted, as I pointed at her.

"I'd better go," Diamond said, as she looked in Trent's direction.

"Yeah, if you enjoy breathing and don't want to be in a casket sometime next week you'll do just that," I said, as I headed to me and Trent's bedroom.

"Diamond, I'm sorry. Lyric didn't mean that," Trent said before she marched out of the front door.

"Don't apologize to her, I did mean that, and if you keep it up, I'll put you in a casket too," I yelled as I walked into my closet.

After I folded the boxes I had gotten from the garage, I grabbed everything that was at arm's length and shoved it into the biggest box. When that box was full, I filled the other boxes and tried to close them. With only three boxes of clothes and one box of shoes, I still had a closet full of things that I needed to pack. There was no way all of this stuff was going to fit in Boogies sports car. After figuring out which boxes I wanted to take, I opened my closet door only to see Trent standing in the doorway.

"Who's the guy in the car?"

"Don't you worry about it," I said as I carried the first box out into the living room.

"So you bring a man to my house, and you think its okay?" He said as I carried the second box into the living room.

"Trent, I just caught you in our house with a woman. How do you think I feel about that?" I yelled as I started crying. "The guy in the car is Boogie, my childhood friend. We invited him to the wedding, but he was away in the military. It just so happens that he's in town for a few.., wait a minute, I shouldn't be explaining myself to you. Go to hell Trent," I shouted as I stacked one box on top of the other and walked out onto the porch.

"So you're leaving?" He asked.

"What does it look like," I replied as I stomped down the sidewalk and up to Boogie's car.

Boogie was startled when he looked up. He'd been looking down at the user manual for his new car and had the music turned up, so he had no idea of what was going on. He immediately got out of the car and opened the trunk, but it still had a lot of his bags and boxes in it. "Will these boxes fit in the back seat?" I asked. Boogie quickly opened the door and adjusted the seat on the passenger side of the car. Both boxes fit, but there wasn't any more room for anything else.

Trent looked at me as I got into the car and closed the door. He could no longer see me because of the tint on the windows. Since Boogie had never cut the car off, he switched the gear from park to drive, and we drove away. I wiped my eyes with the sleeves of my hoodie as I watched Trent look in the direction that the car was headed in.

When we'd pulled back onto Stone Dale Court, Trent had called me six times, and I'd sent Latria an extra-long text message and told her what happened. After Boogie shut the engine off we got out of the car and took the boxes inside of the house. He didn't stay long after that because he had a date with some girl he'd met at the gas station. I walked him to the door and thanked him for always being a friend to me. We hugged and then he left.

After I took a long shower, I went to my old room and got in bed. I debated on calling Mont to tell him what happened, but I decided not to. Instead, I put my phone on silent and watched it light up as Latria; Trent and Jason called, and text messaged me. I felt drained and regretted not fighting Diamond tonight. *"I should've at least slapped her,"* I thought to myself as I drifted off.

10

Sick and Tired

In no time, an entire month had passed, and I was adjusting well to sleeping in my old bed. Trent was calling, at least ten times a day and I still wasn't answering his calls. His voice messages sounded sad, and he even let Tia leave me a few messages. I couldn't listen to them, I missed Tia way more than Trent and thought about going back home but I didn't. I wasn't ready to talk to him, and I still couldn't believe that he had the audacity to have Diamond in our house. There was no telling what he'd been up to since I'd been gone. I didn't think I could ever forgive him for this and at the moment, I hadn't been back home to get the rest of my things. I told myself that I was going to stop by every day, but decided not to when I thought of Trent having another woman in our house. I couldn't handle sticking my key in the door again and seeing him with someone else.

I feared that I would go crazy and hurt or even kill Trent. The last thing I wanted to do was go to jail; I wasn't trying to be anybody's bitch. Besides, staying at mom's house had been beneficial to both of us. I'd been helping her and Ron out around the house, and I even dropped off a few cakes to some of their clients. With Thanksgiving approaching Mom and Ron's catering service were getting a lot of orders. It was a good thing that I'd been staying busy because I wanted to call Mont. I talked to Jason more since I'd left home but no one could ever take Mont's place.

With Boogie leaving the Saturday after Thanksgiving, I knew that it was going to be hard for me to resist calling Mont for sure. I wouldn't have anyone to talk to in the daytime except Jason. It felt like we were in a long distance relationship. Jason even called me his girlfriend, but I had to remind him that a married woman couldn't be his girlfriend. He didn't like that and insisted on calling me his sweet. I'd been called boo, babe, and baby, but never sweet. This was different, and I had to admit, I liked this term of endearment.

As mom and Ron started getting things ready for Thanksgiving, I felt down because I was going to miss having my first Thanksgiving dinner in my house. It was a good thing that no one from our family was coming home because I didn't want them to know that I'd left home already. I was embarrassed with the way things were turning out with me and Trent's marriage. I wanted to tell my sister Raven what happened, but I didn't want to relive what had happened again. I knew that my secrets were safe with Boogie, Mont, Latria, and Mom so I planned on telling no one else.

With absolutely nothing to do, I called Boogie over, and we spent the entire day together. We watched a few Spike Lee movies, made root beer floats, and even played a few rounds of UNO. It felt good being with a man that didn't want anything else from me other than my friendship. After he had beaten the pants off of me in UNO, we sat on the front porch.

We sat in silence for a while and watched the traffic go by like we did when we were teenagers. Eventually, I started a conversation because my mind was flooded with thoughts of Trent.

"So what do you miss the most from our teenage days?" I asked, as my eyes followed a black pick-up truck that was passing.

"Umm, I'd have to say my braces," he responded with a chuckle.

"Are you serious? You almost cried the same day you got them, and you even tried to take them out with a butter knife," I laughed.

"Yeah, those things hurt like hell, but the girls seemed to like them, and they liked me even more once my teeth straightened out," he confessed.

While discussing his braces, Boogie told me about the time that one of his rubber bands flew out of his mouth and hit a girl that sat across from him smack dab in the middle of her forehead. I hadn't heard that story before and laughed so hard that I got dizzy. After we talked about the good times and the bad times from our teenage years, we talked about life in general. He told me about all types of crazy things that happened while he was overseas in the military. I couldn't believe that Boogie had shot people and had almost got blown up while he was overseas. While he told me about his war stories, I was on the edge of my seat. He described things so vividly, and I felt like I was watching a movie.

When the sun began to set Boogie cut his story short, stood up, and brushed the back of his pants off. "I better get going. I've got a hot date tonight, and I can't be late," he said as he winked his eye.

"Who's the lucky girl?" I asked.

"You don't know her."

"I know that smirk," I said as I stood up. "I bet you that I do know her." I laughed as Boogie walked backward and shook his head.

For the next hour, I wondered who was riding shotgun in Boogie's Challenger. I had to get my handsome childhood buddy off my mind, so I called Jason. While I took a warm bubble bath, Trent beeped in several times, and I ignored his calls. As I splashed around, Jason said that he was getting excited and asked if we could video chat later. I agreed because I was horny too. I wished that he was here so we could hook up. I still remembered how he smelled.

We continued to talk as I shaved and cleaned the bathtub out. He was curious about every move I made and kept asking was I done yet. I laughed at how anxious he was. As fine as he was, you'd think that he had all the girls in Hawaii.

When I was finally finished in the bathroom, I slipped on a robe and went downstairs to get a banana. After I put the banana in my room, I walked down the hall and asked my mom if I could borrow her laptop. She pointed it out, and I happily removed it from her desk along with the charger. As soon as I got back in the room, I let Jason know that I had the computer, and we were off of the phone and face to face in no time. After I lit a few candles and turned off the light, I made sure that the bedroom door was locked. I couldn't imagine my mom walking in on me giving Jason a private show.

"I hope you're ready for this," I seductively said, as I turned on some soft music. I didn't know what Jason was doing, but I heard him breathing hard. As I walked in front of the camera, I untied the loose knot in the belt of the robe. Jason watched me carefully as he sat back in a chair. He was shirtless and wore only a pair of navy basketball shorts. His world of curls hung down and around his face as he gave me his undivided attention.

"I hope you know how lucky you are. I've never done anything like this," I confessed, as I reached for the baby oil and squirted a bit into my palms. My bangles clinked and clanked a jingle as I rubbed my palms together. I licked my lips and rubbed the oil on my neck and my breasts. I continued to rub my torso until I needed another squirt of oil. Only, this time, I didn't rub the oil into my hands. I squirted it directly onto my body. As the oil dripped off of my erect nipples, Jason moved closer to his computer screen.

After rubbing baby oil into my skin, I bent over in front of the camera and flipped my hair from one side to the other.

"Damn, Lyric. You don't know how bad I want you right now."

I didn't say anything. I only responded with a sexy smile and left the view of the camera to wipe my hands off and get the banana.

"Wait baby. Where are you going?" He asked.

"I'll be right back," I said as I peeled the banana and folded my robe up.

When I was back in front of the camera, I placed the robe on the floor and knelt down in front of the screen.

"Come closer," I insisted, as he moved closer to the computer screen. "If I were there with you, I would run my fingers through your hair, kiss you, and I'd love to do this," I said, as I put the banana into my mouth and started giving him a preview of my oral skills.

While I slurped and sucked on the banana, I could tell that Jason was losing control. As he fondled himself, he removed his erection from his shorts, and it stood straight up in the air. I had him exactly where I wanted him now, and I put the banana down and slid the laptop over. Then I got on the bed and spread my legs open so he could see my freshly shaved pleasure zone.

"How do you like this view?" I asked in a sultry voice.

"What are you trying to do to me? I need to come back to Virginia right now," he said in a serious tone while he continued to stroke his manhood.

"I wish you were here. I want you inside of me so bad right now," I whined as I inched my fingers closer to my opening and slipped one into my warm wetness.

Jason made a few moaning sounds, and I looked to see that his love had erupted.

"Damn, I need a nap now," he said with a sexy chuckle.

"I'd love to wrap myself around you right now. I wish that you didn't live so far away," I replied, as I closed my legs and repositioned myself in front of the camera.

"Me too. I'd love to be your man. You've got me falling in love with you," Jason said, as he wiped up the love juices that he'd spilled with a nearby towel.

"Falling in love? Jason are you serious?" I boasted.

"I shouldn't have said that," he replied with a dimpled grin.

After giving Jason that show, I felt extra hot, and I opened the window to let in some cool air. For the rest of the night, Jason and I talked and laughed. I liked him, and I couldn't believe that he said he was falling in love with me. I wondered if we were a couple would cheat on me. As it got later and later, I tried to disconnect the call with Jason, but he wouldn't let me go. He insisted that he wanted to sleep with me tonight, and that's exactly what we did.

When I woke up, the first thing I saw was Jason. I don't remember who had fallen asleep on who but he was knocked out. It was crazy; I was even attracted to him when he was asleep. The second thing I noticed was that I was still naked, and the room was cold. My nose felt a bit stopped up as I got up to shut the window and when I tried to swallow my throat was sore. I hoped it was from deep throating that banana and not because I was sick. Whatever the case, I couldn't stand having a sore throat it was pure torture. I wouldn't wish a sore throat on my worst enemy.

Well, maybe I would wish a sore throat on Diamond and Trent too. After I shut the window I called Jason's name, and he didn't budge, so I slipped into my robe, picked up the banana from last night, and headed downstairs. Mom or Ron weren't up yet, so I made a pot of coffee that would satisfy all of our caffeine cravings. After I dropped a few cubes of sugar in my jumbo mug, I added a scoop of creamer and headed back upstairs to Mr. Sleeping Beauty.

To my surprise, Jason was wide awake when I returned.

"Where were you?" He asked, as I got back on the bed and covered up.

"I went downstairs and made some coffee," I answered, as I reached for my coffee mug on the nightstand and took a sip. My throat felt like it was on fire and I must've made a horrible face because Jason asked what was wrong. "I think I have a sore throat from sleeping with the window open. The temperature dropped. I can only imagine how it feels outside because it's cold as hell in here."

"They say hell is hot," Jason joked.

"You know what I mean silly," I said with a straight face.

"If you moved here you wouldn't have to worry about being cold, it's always warm here in Hawaii," he bragged.

"Go ahead, rub it in," I said as I started to feel a little queasy.

After trying to resist the urge to throw up, I drank another sip of coffee and almost threw up on my mom's laptop. I quickly got up and ran across the hall. While I was in the bathroom, I washed my face and brushed my teeth. When I got back in front of the computer, Jason insisted on ending the video call. "Get your rest, I'll call you in a little bit to check on you," he said before he blew me a kiss.

I hated to disconnect the call because Jason was all I had at this very moment. Boogie was probably still on his date from last night, and I didn't want to see Trent at all. The only other person I could think of was my lover-boy Mont. I knew if I called him, he would come running, but something wouldn't let me dial his number. After I shut down the laptop, I wiped it with some Lysol wipes that were under the counter in the bathroom. I didn't want mom to catch whatever it was that I had.

Just as I was about to leave the bathroom, I heard mom's room door open.

"Good morning baby," she said.

"Mom, I don't feel good," I whined as I blew my nose.

"What's wrong?"

"I'm not sure, I threw up this morning, and I think I have a fever. I slept with the window open. I think I have a cold or something," I answered.

"Why in the world would you do that?" She asked while she looked at me like I was crazy.

"I got hot in the middle of the night and needed some air."

"I hope you're not developing hot flashes this early, you're still in your twenties for goodness sake," she said, as she started jumping to conclusions.

"Mom, I'm sure it's not hot flashes. I just got a little hot; that's all," I confirmed.

"Well, I'll bring you some medicine. Get back in the bed and make sure that window is closed."

"Yes ma'am," I said as I marched back to my room and got in the bed.

A few minutes later mom bought some warm tea and two slices of cheese toast. After downing the tea, I ate the cheese toast slowly to make sure that it agreed with my stomach. At the moment it did, so I covered up and went back to sleep. I slept for a few hours and woke up with a runny nose. After looking around the room, I saw that there was no Kleenex in sight. When I stood up to get some tissue, I felt dizzy and nauseated.

I made it to the bathroom just in time, because I had to throw up again. I didn't know what was wrong with me, but I felt horrible. I wasn't up for any conversation, but when my cell phone rang as I settled back into bed, I wondered who it was. After screening the call, I saw that I'd missed a call from Boogie, and I called him back. I listened as he told me about his date. I kept dozing off and missed out on some of the good parts, but he didn't even realize it because he was doing all the talking.

From what I did hear. It sounded like Boogie was in love too. Was love in the air or something? While he continued to talk about this mystery date of his, I felt like I was about to slip into a coma and suggested that I call him back later on. I never called Boogie back, so he took it upon himself to come and visit me. I woke up when I felt that someone was staring at me. Even though my back was turned and I was buried under a mountain of covers.

I knew it was him before he said anything because I smelled his cologne. He'd worn the same cologne for years.

"Hey Boogie," I said, as I rolled over.

"Dang, you are sick. Your mom told me to come up here. She's downstairs making you some soup right now."

That was weird, I could smell Boogies cologne, but I couldn't smell my mom's soup.

"So you think that you got enough blankets on your bed?" He asked as he pointed to the six blankets.

"No, I could use another one," I said as I sat up and took a sip of water.

"Okay," Boogie said as he opened the closet door, and reached inside for another blanket. As he spread out the blanket and lay it on top of the others, I thanked him. "So what do you think you have? The flu or a virus?"

"I'm not sure, but I know you don't want to catch this bug. I feel like I'm about to kick the bucket," I admitted.

"You're right, if you feel any better later call me," he said as he left the room.

The extra blanket that Boogie put on the bed didn't do any good. I still felt cold, and I couldn't get warm. If I didn't feel any better in the morning, I was going to go to the doctor. Not long after Boogie left, mom came upstairs and bought me some of her homemade chicken soup along with some cold medicine. I was hungry and ate the soup with no problem other than my sore throat. The medicine that she gave me was thicker than honey and very bitter.

After I ate and took the medicine mom suggested that I take a shower and change into some fresh pajamas. I did as she'd suggested and had to admit that I felt a little better, but I couldn't get warm. For the remainder of the evening, I listened to Latria on the phone as she complained and fussed about different things. When I couldn't take any more of Latria's pettiness, I ended the call and text Jason to see what he was up to. He wanted to open a video call, but I didn't have the strength to get up and get the laptop from my mother's room.

The next morning it was freezing and raining cats and dogs. I still felt terrible and knew that I should have gone to the doctor, but I figured going out in the weather would only make me feel worse. So I postponed my trip to the doctor's office and stayed in bed all day again. That evening, I went downstairs and made a cup of tea. When I drank it with no problem, I realized that while I was napping the soreness in my throat had gone away. Now that my throat was better, I knew that I would be able to talk to Jason tonight.

I sent him a quick text message and looked around the kitchen for some more of the cold medicine that my mom had given me last night. As soon as I opened the cabinet I saw it and happily poured a dose of the bitter liquid into a spoon. I chased the cough syrup down with a cup of orange juice and washed the few dishes that were in the sink before I headed back upstairs. I was in such a good mood, I thought about making breakfast for Mom and Ron in the morning.

That night I talked to Jason until we both fell asleep in front of the camera again. I had to admit, I felt like I was falling in love with him too, but I didn't tell him that. When I woke up, I felt fine, until I smelled bacon cooking. I immediately got up and threw up in the toilet. While I was in the bathroom, my cell phone rang, and I picked it up when I saw Latria's name pop up on the caller ID. I answered in between heaves and the first thing Latria said was, "I know what's wrong with you."

"What? You think I've got food poisoning or something?" I asked as I wiped my mouth with the back of my hand and went back to my room.

"Nope. I think that you may be pregnant. I'm going to bring you a test, and we'll find out if you are. I'll be there in five minutes. Don't pee yet, save it for the test," she squealed before she hung up.

I didn't know what to do. I was scared out of my mind. I looked back at the computer screen to Jason sleeping peacefully. Then I tried to think back to my last period, and I couldn't remember. I knew that there could be a possibility that I could very well be pregnant because I hadn't taken a birth control pill for God knows how long. I knew the last person that I'd had sex with was Jason. My knees grew weak as I thought back to the condom breaking the last time that we had sex. I hoped that I wasn't pregnant because if I was, I wasn't sure if Trent or Jason would be the baby's father. Trent and I had only gotten busy one time before Jason came. I crossed my fingers and looked at Jason one last time before I disconnected the video call.

11

Pink or Blue

Latria was right, I was pregnant. I knew something was wrong with me, but I honestly thought I had the flu. It was November, and the weather was changing. I couldn't believe that I was pregnant, in the middle of all of this madness. With most of my things packed in boxes back at home, I made my mind up that I would tell Trent today. Lord knows the last thing I needed right now was a baby. Of course, I had Tia, but she wasn't really my child. I loved her like I gave birth to her, though. Tia could do things for herself and wasn't totally dependent on me. I knew that having a baby would not only change my life, but it would change my body too. I wished that I would have taken my birth control pills like I was supposed to.

Since the test confirmed that I was pregnant, I put on my big girl panties and faced reality. This had to be God's plan for making me slow down and having an abortion was not an option. Deep down I hoped that this pregnancy would make me and Trent's relationship stronger. The first person I told was my mom, and she was overjoyed. After getting advice from her and Latria, I knew that it was time to call Trent and tell him that I was coming over.

Before I dialed Trent's number, I sent Jason a text message that read, "Sorry for ending our camera call earlier, something came up, and I've got to take care of the situation. Until then, please don't call me. I will try to call you later tonight." He didn't respond, so I assumed that he was still asleep. With Jason out of my hair for a little while, I took a deep breath and dialed Trent's number. He answered on the very first ring and told me how much he missed me before I could say anything. When he asked me to come over and talk I agreed and told him that I would be over within the next hour. Just as I was about to walk out the door, mom called me into the living room and said a prayer for me and Trent's marriage. When I left Stone Dale Court, I prayed to myself as I drove the familiar route home.

I drove in silence and tried to think positive thoughts as I wondered if Diamond had been back over. When I pulled into the driveway, I noticed that everything still looked the same as I put the car in park and got out. Just as I walked onto the porch, Trent opened the door, and I went inside. I didn't see Tia, but I saw a few of her doll babies sitting on the couch.

I wondered where she was until he broke the silence by saying, "Tia's at my mother's house. I figured that we should be alone to talk just in case things got out of hand."

"Oh, I thought I was going to see her," I said, as I took off my coat and breathed in the familiar smell of home.

I didn't know it, but I had missed that smell.

"I'm ready to talk, but I guess you already knew that because I called you," I said, as I sat down on the couch.

"Baby, I'm sorry. I'm ready to talk, I mean I'm ready to listen," he replied, as he sat down beside me.

"I'm going to be honest with you Trent, I'm not sure if I'm ready to come back home yet because you really hurt me. I love you, and I want us to be a happy family, me, you, Tia, and the baby."

"Me, you, Tia, and the baby?" Trent asked.

Even though he was in the dog house and knew that I didn't want him to touch me, he picked me up and swung me around.

"Put me down," I hissed, as he followed my instructions.

"I'm sorry, I'm just so excited that we're going to have a baby together. We've got to tell Tia," he said excitedly, as he kissed me on my cheek.

Instead of wiping the kiss off, I let it soak in because I knew that I was going to move back in within the week. After I told him the exciting news, he got down on his knees and apologized again, swore he would remain faithful, and then he confessed his love for our unborn child.

After accepting his apology, I agreed that I would ride with him to his mom's house to tell her and Tia the good news. On the way to the car, Trent attempted to hold my hand. Only, I didn't want to hold his hand just yet, so I didn't clasp hands with him. When he saw that he'd gotten rejected, he gave me a little space, but he still opened the car door for me.

As we drove over to his mother's house, we discussed baby names and even talked about where we would have the baby shower. I don't know how he did it, but I realized that Trent and I were holding hands before we pulled up in his mom's driveway. When we parked, he smoothly reached over and pulled my face towards his and we shared our first makeup kiss. There was a little bit of tongue involved with a lot of passion, I wanted to pull away but couldn't. I guess I wanted this kiss just like he wanted it.

"I'll get the door for you," he announced as he got out the car and opened my car door. "Thank you," I said as I got out of the car and stepped onto the concrete. After he shut the door, he reached down and took my hand. This time, I didn't reject him and let him hold my hand. We held hands tightly until we walked onto the porch and he rang the doorbell.

"Grammy, someone is at the door," I heard Tia yell.

"It's me baby, open the door," Trent shouted with a grin.

"Grammy, it's Daddy. I can see him. Can I open it?"

"No, I'm coming, I'll get it," Trent's mom said.

I continued to stand behind Trent as we entered the house. Tia hadn't seen me yet. "Aww, it's so nice to see you Lyric," Trent's mother said, as she leaned over and gave me a hug. When Tia noticed that I was there, she jumped into my arms. I'm glad that I have good reflexes if I didn't Tia would have been on the floor. As we hugged each other, Trent's mother invited us into the kitchen where she was prepping food for Thanksgiving dinner tomorrow. As we sat down at the table, Tia sat on my lap and played with my bangles on my arm.

"Mom and Tia, we have something to tell you," Trent said.

"What is it son, I'm getting too old for surprises?" She said with a smile.

I think that his mom already knew that I was pregnant. Older people knew that kind of stuff, I don't know how but they did. I think it was like a sixth sense or something.

"Lyric is pregnant," he said.

His mom put her hands high in the air and yelled, "Thank you, Jesus."

After she raised the roof and clapped her hands, she walked over and gave us each a hug. When she hugged me, she whispered, "I knew it. The way you were glowing when you walked in gave it away."

While Trent's mother was whispering in my ear, Tia shouted, "I'm going to be a big sister," then she jumped down off of my lap and did a mini-cartwheel in the kitchen. "I'm going to be a big sister," she shouted again, as she ran around the house. While they celebrated, I secretly hoped that the baby wasn't Jason's. I knew that we only hooked up a few times, but all it took was one time, and the condom did break, so I tried to hide the worry that was building inside by asking for a glass of wine.

Trent looked at me and said, "You can't have any wine, you're pregnant."

"Yes she can, it's not going to hurt the baby. I used to drink wine at least twice a week when I was pregnant with you," his mother confessed.

"Oh, really!" Trent replied to his mother. "Well pour me a glass too, because this is definitely something worth celebrating."

"Can I have some wine too daddy?" Tia asked.

"You're too young to have wine darling. I'll tell you what. You can have some apple juice in a wine glass."

"Okay daddy," Tia replied with a smile as she settled back into my lap.

Deep down I had to admit, I was happy that there was a little person growing inside of me. As I wondered if the baby would be a boy or a girl, the thought of who the baby may look bombarded my mind and I began to feel sick. In spite of the fact that I was starting to feel ill, I would remain hopeful that Trent would be the father. I knew that I would lose him for good if he knew that I'd slept with someone else. At that moment, I realized that I didn't even care anymore because of the thought of finding Diamond in our house made me angry all over again. If the baby was Trent's or not I was going to let him sign the birth certificate and keep it moving.

The same day that I shared the baby news with Trent and Tia, I moved back home. After we left Trent's mother's house, we went to Stone Dale Court and picked up my things. As we were putting my belongings into the car, I saw Boogie drive by. He waved and blew the horn at us. When I waved back, I had to remember to call and share the good news with him before someone else could tell him. It didn't take long to put my stuff in the car, before I left I gave my mother a big hug and thanked her for taking care of me. As we backed out of the driveway, mom waved and watched us as we drove away.

On that same evening, we had cocoa from Starbucks and went shopping for a Christmas tree. After finding a Christmas tree farm on the outskirts of town, we selected a tree that would fit our home best.

Since we didn't have a truck, we paid the owner of the lot to deliver our tree. He followed us as we drove home. I didn't realize that the tree was so big until it was positioned in the corner of the living room. It was a good thing we didn't pick a bigger tree because it would not have fit without trimming it and nobody wanted to do that.

Tia was ready to add decorations to the tree and drug me into the garage to find ornaments. There were two boxes marked "Christmas Decorations" on a shelf in the garage. As I wondered where the ladder was, Trent joined us in the garage and said, "I hope you're not thinking about getting those boxes down from there."

"I can get it," I said as I climbed onto the first step of the ladder.

"Lyric, please. Let me, I don't want anything to happen to you or the baby."

"Oh, I didn't think about it like that," I said, as I stepped off of the ladder.

He then climbed the steps of the ladder and got the boxes that were on the shelf. Tia and I moved out of his way and followed close behind him as he set the boxes on the floor around the Christmas tree. The ornaments that were in the boxes were the traditional red, green, and gold colors and I was fine with that. While I sat and unwrapped the cords of the Christmas lights, Trent removed the broken ornaments out of the box and straightened out the hooks.

After all the lights were untangled, we began to wrap the tree. Trent had to go back in the garage and get the ladder because we couldn't reach the top of the tree without it. Tia placed ornaments on the lower half of the tree; I put them in the middle and Trent placed the ornaments on the top of the tree. When it was time to put the star on the tree, Trent carefully followed Tia up the ladder and let her put the star on top. The tree was gorgeous. I took a few pictures of the tree and sent them to my email address. I would see if I could get some Christmas cards made using this image the next time I went to the store.

That night we ordered Tia's favorite pizza. While we waited for the delivery guy to show up, I got Tia ready for bed. When she was squeaky clean, I let her pick out the pajamas that she wanted to wear, and we headed towards the smell of the pizza in the kitchen. After only eating one slice, Tia started to fall asleep at the table.

"She's had a long and exciting day," Trent said from across the table.

"Yes, she has. She'll sleep well tonight," I said as Trent scooped her into his strong arms.

"Go ahead and eat, I'm going to lay her down, I'll be right back."

"Alright," I replied as I grabbed another slice of pizza.

"I'm going to run a nice hot bath. Can you meet me in the bathroom in ten minutes?" He asked.

"I certainly can, that's just what I need."

While Trent walked off in the direction of our bedroom, I finished eating my slice of pepperoni pizza and went to kiss Tia good night. I kissed her on the top of her head and made sure that her closet light was on. I'd only been gone for a while, but I remembered that she preferred leaving her closet light on instead of plugging in the nightlight. I sat on the floor beside her bed until I heard the water in the bathroom stop running.

On my way back to the kitchen, I folded the pizza box and tossed it in the trash can. After I turned off the lights, I walked into the bedroom. Immediately, I smelled a sweet fragrance that wasn't familiar at all. Candles were lit all around the bathroom, and the tub was full of bubbles, I couldn't wait to get in. "Take your clothes off," he whispered just as I stepped across the threshold of the bathroom. I did as he said and stripped. For a brief second, I stood in front of the mirror and adored my flat stomach. I wondered if it would look like this after I had the baby.

Before I could think of any other baby related thoughts, Trent took me by the hand and helped me into the tub. For a second, I thought that he was going to join me until he reached under the cabinet and retrieved a brand new body sponge. That night Trent bathed me like a Queen. I felt like a million bucks as I lay on the fresh sheets. We slept in the nude, but we didn't have sex. He only held me in his arms and didn't let me go.

The next morning when I woke up, Trent still had his arms wrapped around me. His head was buried in the nape of my neck.

"Trent, wake up, it's Thanksgiving Day, and I don't have anything to take to your mother's house for dinner."

"Aww baby, it's alright. She knows that we were going through some things and isn't expecting us to bring anything. You really made her day yesterday with that baby news. I promise it will be okay," he replied as he yawned.

"Did you tell your mom that you cheated on me?" I asked as I sat up in the bed.

"Not exactly, she doesn't need to know everything. All I told her is that we got into an argument and that you left," he answered.

"What? Now she's probably going to think that I'm petty and that I'll walk out on my marriage over something as simple as an argument. I can't believe you," I hissed as I got up and slipped on an oversized t-shirt.

"Lyric what did you want me to tell my mom?" He asked as he followed me into the bathroom.

"I want you to tell her the same thing that you told my mom. You told me that you messed up and had a weak moment. You should've told your mom that very same thing. Don't make it look like I left home because of something that I did, because I didn't. You screwed up, not me."

"You're right. I'll make sure I tell her today. I'm sorry baby. Do you forgive me?" He asked as he stood there naked.

"I guess so. Just don't make me look like the bad guy."

The first day of December I had a scheduled doctor's appointment. Trent insisted that he go with me, so we dropped Tia off at his mother's house and headed downtown. After a quick fifteen minute drive, we pulled into the parking lot and parked. When we got out of the car, we went inside of the building, and I signed in. As soon as we sat down, the nurse called my name, and I followed her while Trent followed me. The first thing I had to do was urinate in a cup. While I was doing my business in the small bathroom, Trent waited for me in a chair in the hallway.

When I was all done, I walked out of the bathroom and handed the nurse my cup of warm urine. As she checked the urine, she confirmed the obvious. "Congratulation Mrs. Morrison. You are indeed pregnant," she said with a smile. I gave her a smile back, as I sat down in a chair that looked like it belonged in a classroom. I looked at Trent as she tied a tourniquet around my arm and felt my veins. When she found a fat juicy one she rubbed the spot with an alcohol pad and inserted a thin needle into my arm.

I felt a small pinch, and that was it. The nurse then filled up a few vials of blood and took the needle out of my vein. After applying a cotton ball over the small drop of blood that was on my arm, she took a Band-Aid out of the pack and stuck it on the spot where she had inserted the needle. "Alright, let's weigh you and get your blood pressure, then you and your husband can go to that room on the left and wait for the doctor," she said as she pointed to the examination room. "Alright," I said anxiously as I took my shoes off before I stepped up onto the scale.

There was no guessing involved because the scale was digital and not one of those old school ones that you had to slide the metal bar across. The number 146 flashed on the screen, and I took a deep breath. I'd gained six pounds since the last time I weighed three weeks ago. After the nurse wrote down my weight in my chart, she hooked me up to an automatic blood pressure cuff. When the cuff was done squeezing my arm it deflated, and the nurse reported that my blood pressure was normal and showed us to the examination room.

I sat on the table and flipped through a Women's Health magazine while Trent sat in a chair next to a stack of birth control pamphlets. We waited in silence until the doctor came in and introduced herself. After getting checked out by the doctor, I learned that I was on the right track considering that I'd gained the six pounds. I wasn't happy about that, and the doctor mentioned that I could start walking a few days a week to maintain my weight. Before I left the doctor gave me a due date of mid-June and a prescription for some prenatal vitamins. After Trent paid the lady at the front desk for my visit, we headed to the pharmacy to get my vitamins.

That following day Jason called me and I didn't answer. I wanted to talk to him, but I let the call go to voicemail. I was so proud of myself. I liked Jason and not answering his calls were a sign that I did have a little self-control. With Melody's birthday getting closer with each passing day I thought of Jason less and less. One day he sent a text message out of the blue asking for nude pictures, I ignored his request because my stomach was getting bigger and it was very noticeable.

I didn't want him to know that I was pregnant. After he'd told me that he was falling in love with me, I didn't know how he would react to this baby news. The last thing I needed was for him to show up at my house uninvited like Mont did. If he knew I was pregnant, I feared that he would ask me if the baby was his. I hoped that Jason would get a clue and realize that I didn't want to talk to him anymore. Now that Trent and I were back together I wanted to do right. I didn't want to be the one to break up our marriage by being promiscuous, so I had to ignore his calls and messages.

I think that it would be safe to say that I let Mont go too. He still called and sent text messages that I ignored. Unlike Jason, Mont was my ultimate weakness and I couldn't resist him when we were face to face. No man had ever made me feel the way that he did when we were together sexually. I tried not to think about him, but my bangles were a constant reminder because he'd bought me so many of them. I thought about taking them off again, but every time I heard them jingle it made me think of the song jingle bells, and it kept me in good spirits. With Melody's birthday approaching, I had to have something that would keep my mind off of her. That's the main reason that I decided to keep wearing them. It was a crazy thought, but I wondered if Diamond sold bangles at her jewelry store.

12

Changes

Christmas was over and done with, and I couldn't be happier. The gigantic tree that we picked out at the Christmas tree farm had been stripped of the precious glass ornaments and thrown outside. With the decorations put in the boxes and placed back on the top shelf in the garage, the living room was almost back to normal. The smell of the tree lingered in the living area until Trent opened the windows and let in some fresh air. I couldn't stand the smell anymore; it was crazy that it happened all of a sudden. I was fine up until a few hours ago.

After the floors were swept and cleaned the stinky smell was gone. I never wanted another live Christmas tree again; the tree had shed all over the place, and prickly needles were everywhere. While Tia and Trent cleaned up the living room, I lay on the bed with my head spinning. This baby was wearing me out. My feet were swollen, and my senses were all out of whack. I smelled things that I'd never noticed before. The smell of cinnamon burned my nose and made me gag. I couldn't go anywhere without sneezing, throwing up, or gagging.

Not only were my senses out of control, but I'd also gained another five pounds, and it had only been thirty days since my last doctor's visit. I didn't know what I was going to do if I kept gaining weight like this. I didn't want to look like Miss. Piggy at the end of my pregnancy. I had to stop eating so much and start exercising, like the doctor suggested. All of my clothes were getting too tight, and I needed to shop for maternity clothes as soon as possible. I'd been cooped up inside of the house and I'd only been wearing Trent's pajamas and oversized t-shirts.

As I lay on the bed thinking about my growing list of ailments, my stomach started to itch like crazy. I tried my best not to scratch it as I thought about the risk of having stretch marks. Mom suggested that I rub cocoa butter all over my stomach each time I get out of the shower to prevent stretch marks, but I used the last bit last night. Since I didn't have anymore, I decided that I would make a list and possibly do a little shopping sometime this week.

When I got up, I squeezed into a pair of stretch jeans and a one size fits all sweatshirt. It was a good thing that the sweater was big because I couldn't fasten my pants. I zipped them up halfway and hoped that I didn't look awkward. After I put my hair in a quick ponytail, I grabbed my keys and purse. On my way out the door, Tia asked if she could tag along. I told her that she could go, and Trent insisted that he go too. That was fine with me because I knew that I had a special stop to make.

Today was the first day I'd been out since the doctor's visit, I planned on going to Melody's grave because today was her birthday. If it weren't her birthday, I probably would have ended up staying in the house today too. I felt lazy; this baby was sucking the life out of me. I didn't have any extra energy, I didn't even like to talk on the phone. If mom or Latria wanted to chat, they had to come over. I didn't get up to unlock the door for them either. They used the hidden key that was in the planter outside of the front door to let themselves in. When they came, they usually bought me goodies. I looked forward to their visits because I hadn't heard a thing from Dana since she got engaged a week after my wedding. I really missed my friend and wondered what she was up to. I knew that she had to be thinking about me because this time of the year was usually tough for me and she knew that. She was the one who was always there handing me a fresh box of Kleenex.

As I thought about Dana, I touched the bangles that she'd given me. They were so pretty. Then I thought about all of the crazy times that we'd endured, I knew that I had to call her soon. Plus, I had to tell her that I was expecting. I hope she'd agree to come to the baby shower, it was hard enough getting her to be in our wedding. I knew that I may be pushing it by inviting her to the baby shower, but the only way I'll know if she'll come is to ask her. All she can say is yes or no.

While my thoughts drifted away from my old sweetheart, I'd realized that I'd made it through the holidays without breaking down. Considering that today was Melody's birthday, I felt fine emotionally. With all of this thinking going on I hadn't noticed that we were parked in front of the flower shop. After Trent unlocked the doors, we all got out and went inside. When my old friend saw me enter through the glass door, she shouted, "The usual my dear?" "Yes ma'am," I replied with a smile. While she prepared my order, I introduced Tia and Trent to her. Since we were the only customers in the shop we discussed my pregnancy and I shared the due date with her. On our way out of the door, I went back and gave her a hug while I held in a sneeze. The flowers were getting to me, and I hadn't even been in the shop for ten minutes.

"She's nice," Trent said as we drove away from the flower shop. "Yes she is, her sister is buried a few graves away from Melody. I'm going to put a few of these flowers on her grave today too," I said while I looked out of the window. My throat felt thick, almost like I had drunk a glass of molasses. I wanted to tell Trent to turn around, but I couldn't utter a word. As he continued to drive and hum along with the song on the radio, we got closer to the cemetery and the closer we got, the harder it was for me to breathe. I wasn't sure if I was having a panic attack, but my chest felt constricted.

"I can't go," I blurted out in sobs. Trent hit the brakes and pulled over to the side of the road. "Mommy Lyric, are you okay?" Tia cried, from the back seat. I didn't answer her, I only opened the car door and squatted down on the side of the car. I started throwing up as Trent came to my side. "We don't have to go to the cemetery. I can take the flowers later for you. I'm taking you back home," he said, as he pulled me up off of the cold ground. I didn't argue with him as he turned the car around and headed back home.

For the remainder of the afternoon, I lay on the couch wrapped in a cashmere throw blanket. Tia didn't leave my side as we watched the Disney channel. Trent cooked a few grilled cheese sandwiches and a can of tomato soup for us. We munched on our sandwiches as he left to take the flowers to the cemetery.

"Don't forget to put a few of the flowers on Emma's grave," I said as he walked closer to the front door. "Oh and I need some cocoa butter too."

"Okay, I'll be back in an hour, or so."

"Daddy, can I have some cotton candy?" Tia asked.

"Sure pumpkin, if I can find some I will get it for you," he said as he left.

It took Trent three hours to return; I wondered if he made a pit stop. It should have only taken him an hour or so to return home. I kept my thoughts to myself and smiled at him as he came in and handed Tia a bag of blue cotton candy. "Thank you, Daddy," she said, as she untied the red and white striped twist tie on the bag. While she enjoyed the sugary sweet treat, I gave Trent a good look over and noticed that his slacks were wrinkled. It looked as if they had been balled up. I wondered if Trent stopped by to give Diamond some end of the year loving before the New Year came in.

While thoughts of how Trent's pants got so wrinkled floated around in my head, Tia stuffed a puff of cotton candy into my mouth.

"That's good," I said as I opened my mouth for another piece. Tia was happy to share the cotton candy with me.

"Mommy Lyric, can the baby taste the candy?" She asked.

"I'm not sure, what do you think honey?" I asked as Trent fumbled with his phone.

"Of course, the baby can taste it, give Mommy Lyric some more of that candy," he added.

As I opened my mouth to ask who he was texting, Tia shoved a huge glob of blue cotton candy in my mouth and said, "This is for the baby."

As the candy dissolved, I laughed and decided not to spoil the moment by worrying about Trent and his phone.

"So what do you want to do for your birthday tomorrow?" He asked as he put his phone in his pocket.

"Maybe the three of us could go out to dinner and go to the maternity store to shop for some maternity clothes."

"That sounds like a plan, as of right now I don't have to work tomorrow."

"Great, it'll just be the three of us," I responded, as Tia and I finished off her bag of cotton candy.

That New Year's Eve was the first one I'd slept through in a long time. I didn't know when the countdown happened in time square or anything. All I knew is that I woke up on the couch with Tia sleeping right beside me. I hoped that she didn't have an accident as I reached down and felt the couch. With the sun peeking in through the shades, I woke Tia up so she could use the bathroom.

"Happy birthday beautiful," Trent said as he entered the living room and kissed me on the forehead.

"Thank you darling."

"You and Tia need to get dressed, we have breakfast reservations at that fancy restaurant downtown called A.M."

"Really, I heard a lot of good talk about that place," I replied excitedly, as I headed to the bedroom to get ready.

I heard a buzzing noise when I entered the bedroom, but didn't pay it much attention as I searched for something to wear. As I pulled out a pair of black leggings, I knew that these would be the ones I would wear because they were extra stretchy. I added a cream sweater and a pair of tan *UGG* boots to complete my outfit. It didn't take me long to get dressed. I didn't put on any makeup, I only applied a little lip gloss on my lips and I was ready. Before we headed out to the car, I took Tia into our bathroom and brushed her hair into a ponytail. "Mommy Lyric can I have shiny lips like yours?" She asked. "Yes you can," I answered as I unscrewed the top off of the cocoa butter. I dipped my finger into the creamy concoction and rubbed it onto her lips. Trent laughed as she rubbed her lips together. After he complimented both of us, we were out the door and on our way to breakfast.

Breakfast at A.M. was excellent. My bacon was extra crispy, just how I liked it. I drank two cups of fresh squeezed orange and ordered another before we left. According to Trent the next stop was the nail salon. Since it was so cold, I decided that Tia and I only get manicures. Besides, I was ready to get to the mall to shop for maternity clothes and didn't want to wait for our toes to dry. There were plenty of great sales at the mall, but not in the maternity store. One pair of pants cost almost fifty bucks, and the maternity shirts were just as expensive.

I didn't know how much money Trent was willing to spend today, so I only picked up two pairs of jeans, three shirts, and a few pairs of colored tights that were near the register. After he paid for my maternity clothes, we left the store and walked out into the mall traffic. Right across the way was a big toy store. As soon as Tia saw the giant teddy bear in the window, she asked if she could go inside. He agreed to take her to the toy store, but I just didn't have the energy, so I decided not to go inside with them.

I sat in a group of benches that were situated in the middle of the mall. After about ten minutes of waiting, I decided to walk to the food court and treat myself to a cold lemonade. When I was in line someone tapped me on my shoulder, and I turned around to see Jason. I almost died right in the very spot I stood. "Hello stranger," he said as he bent down and gave me a hug. That's when he saw the baby bump. I was speechless, I'm sure that all the blood had drained from my face, and I was pale as a ghost. "Hi," I murmured as he took me by the hand and pulled me out the line.

I knew that I was in big trouble with him before he even opened his mouth.

"Is this why you've been ignoring me?" He asked, as he looked down at my belly?

"Not really," I answered, as I looked down at his shoes.

"Lyric, look at me. Is that my baby?" He inquired, as he grabbed me by my chin.

I took a deep breath and answered, "There is a good chance that it very well may be Jason."

"So that's why you cut me off. I hope you're not planning on having an abortion."

"Does it look like I'm planning on having an abortion standing here with all of these bags of maternity clothes?" I sarcastically asked.

"I didn't know what was in those bags. I've never heard of Mommy Maternity," he replied, as he looked down at the bags I was carrying.

"Jason, I'm here with my husband and stepdaughter. They're in the toy store right around the corner. I can't risk them seeing me with you," I said as I started to walk back towards the lemonade stand.

"I'll be here for three more days, I'm staying at the same place as last time. I'm in room 329. I'm going to text you later. Please respond," he whispered while he followed me and stood behind me in line.

"Jason, I'm not going to promise you that I'll come by, but I will respond if you send me a text message later," I said before I saw Trent and Tia coming around the corner.

While Jason stood behind me in the line like he was going to order a lemonade, Trent and Tia joined me. I got so nervous that I could hardly breathe. "Let me get those bags for you honey," Trent said as he took my bags and went to sit at one of the tables in the food court. Tia stayed with me and stared at Jason standing so close behind me. When I noticed Tia staring, I told her to turn around. "Mommy Lyric, he's pretty," she said as I laughed and turned to look at Jason. The both of us smiled at each other and then I looked over to see what Trent was doing. I wasn't surprised at all when I saw him with his eyes glued to the screen of his cell phone.

As time went on and the weather warmed up, I started replying to more and more of Jason's messages. Even though I'd never gone to his hotel room that day back in January, he still hadn't given up on our so-called relationship. He was happy to be back in the picture and asked a lot of questions about the pregnancy. Just the other day he asked me to send him a picture of my bare belly, and I'd fulfilled his request. We even talked on the phone a few times, not about anything sexual, our conversations were only related to my pregnancy. I had to admit I was starting to feel a little guilty about this whole baby situation, and it didn't help that I still had my suspicions about Trent cheating. I started to reach out to Mont to see if he had any more information but I didn't. I couldn't take any more stress, I was nearing the end of my pregnancy, and my entire body was swollen. I'd gained over 50lbs. I was so fat that I couldn't even fit my wedding ring, and I couldn't stand looking in the mirror.

A few weeks before I was due to deliver, Mom threw us a baby shower. It was held in the reception hall at her church. A lot of church members showed up with gifts that I didn't even know. Of course, Latria came and to my surprise, Dana came too. She didn't RSVP, so I wasn't expecting her to show up. I got to meet her new fiancée; she was pretty, but she had a lot of visible tattoos and wore a nose ring. I hoped that this worked out for Dana. She didn't seem to have any luck when it came to women. As she bought in lots of colorful gift bags, I couldn't help but wonder if Dana had stolen my baby's stuff. I put the thought in the back of my head as the shower started, and the games began.

I never knew that baby showers could be so fun, I think that I enjoyed it mainly because I was the center of attention. When it was time to open the gifts, everyone gathered around. As I unwrapped the gifts, Ron and Trent started packing them into our car because it was almost time for the shower to be over. As the guest started clearing out, some people waved goodbye from a distance, others gave me hugs, or rubbed my belly before they left. I saw Dana when she and her girlfriend walked out, a part of me wanted to run after her and give her a hug.

I pretended to go to the bathroom and watched them out the bathroom window. When Dana turned around and headed back to the building without her girlfriend, I came out of the bathroom. When I looked out the door, I saw my mom was talking to Dana and pointing in the direction of the restroom. Without them seeing me, I ducked back in and waited for Dana to peek her head inside the door. When the door opened, I pretended as if I was about to walk out.

"Oh, Dana. Hey, I thought you'd left."

"I did, but I wanted to tell you goodbye first," she responded, as she reached into the baggy cargo pocket of her pants.

"This is for you," she said, as she held a box in her hand.

I smiled as I took the box from Dana's hand. When I looked inside, I knew that I couldn't accept this gift.

"I can't take this," I argued as I handed the bangle back to her.

"You don't have a choice, because I'm not taking it back," she protested as she placed the box on the counter.

We both stood in silence for a moment until I gave in.

"Alright, alright. I'll take it," I said as I added the bangle with the others on my arm.

Dana smiled and gave me an awkward hug. I pulled her close to me as I could without hurting my stomach and hugged her back.

"I love you, Dana."

"I love you too Lyric," she replied as she pulled away. Then she said, "I'm here if you need me, remember that."

Then she left me all alone in the bathroom. Before going back out to what was left of the baby shower, I wet a paper towel, wiped my face, and threw the empty bangle box in the trash.

Everything was almost cleaned up and there was so much food leftover. The church ladies insisted that I go home and that they would finish cleaning up. After I agreed to do just that, I packed three carryout trays to take home. The shower was a memorable event, and the photographer took lots of pictures. Considering that we didn't know what the sex of the baby was, we received baby items that were neutral in color, as well as gift certificates, and tons of diapers. I didn't know who was more excited, Mom, Trent, or Tia. I couldn't lie, I was excited too, but I was exhausted, and the thoughts of laying eyes on my baby was about to drive me insane. *"Would the baby look like Trent or Jason?"* That question echoed inside of my head for the entire ride home.

Trent and I were blessed with so much stuff we couldn't fit everything in one car. Mom and Ron followed us home with the rest of the baby's things in the back of her Land Rover. When we pulled into the driveway, I walked to the mailbox and found a card inside. There wasn't a name or even a stamp on the outside, so I know that someone personally opened our mailbox and put this envelope inside. I was torn between opening the envelope because it reminded me of the envelope I'd gotten when I was a teenager, notifying me that I should visit the health department.

Without even thinking about it for another second, I tore open the envelope to find a gift card for $1500 to a baby boutique downtown. I knew that this was Mont's doing. He'd definitely had the balls to do something like this. This had to be one of the sweetest things that he'd ever done. I was thankful and decided that I would call him as soon as I got a moment alone. I guess he knew that I was pregnant. Maybe he saw me out, and about somewhere and I didn't see him. Whatever the case, I had to thank him because he really didn't have to do this.

That night I didn't get a moment alone because Trent and Ron started painting the nursery. I was left to entertain Mom and Tia. All I had to do was turn the television on, and Tia was out of my hair. After Mom and I put all the windows up in the house, we munched on the leftovers from the baby shower. I couldn't keep the secret of the gift card, so I leaned in to tell mom about it, and she nearly choked on a meatball. Her eyes stretched as she smiled and looked over her shoulder to see where Tia was. "That was really nice of him. Have you thanked him yet?"

"No, I wanted to call him, but it looks like I'm going to have to send him a text message."

"Well, go ahead and send it, so he'll know that you got the card out of the mailbox," she whispered.

While looking down the hallway mom made sure the coast was clear while I sent Mont a simple text that read, "Thank you for the gift card." Not even ten seconds later, he responded with a text message that read, "You're welcome, I'd do anything to keep a smile on your face." As much as I wanted to respond to his message, I didn't. I felt butterflies in the pit of my stomach as I thought about him, and I felt like I was floating. I wasn't sure if I was having contractions or if I was high on the fumes of the paint. I didn't know what was going on, but I liked this feeling so much that I wished I could bottle it and sell it.

13

Ready or Not

That same night, I woke up from my sleep in so much pain, and I thought I was going to die. I cried out for Trent, and he jumped out of bed and turned on the light.

"Is it time?"

"I think so" I said as I attempted to stand up but couldn't.

"Alright baby, let me call mom and tell her that we're going to drop Tia off," he said, as he grabbed his cell phone.

While he talked to his mom, my water broke as I stood up and leaned against my nightstand.

"My water just broke Trent; I think that we need to go straight to the hospital. Tell your mom to meet us. She can pick Tia up from there," I said as I immediately felt a sharp pain in my pelvis.

"Lyric, please don't leave me like Anna did. I love you so much," he said softly, as he hugged me.

That's when I realized that I could die while giving birth just like Anna did. That thought scared the shit out of me, and I wanted to get to the hospital faster than ever now.

When we were all loaded in the car, Trent called 911 and notified the operator that he was speeding and that his wife was having a baby. I felt as though I was going to pass out from all the pain that I was in. When we got to the emergency room, Trent ran in and told the lady behind the desk that I was in Labor. I couldn't hear what he said, but I read his lips because the sliding doors to the emergency room had shut behind him when he ran inside. From the passenger seat of the car I watched her jump up from behind the desk and grab a wheelchair.

I'm sure that the lady was moving fast, but it looked like she was moving in slow motion. After Trent opened my car door, his mom pulled up behind us in the emergency department drop off. She helped me out of the car along with the lady from behind the desk. Trent watched in a state of shock as they rolled me away. On the way to the maternity ward, I wondered what was going to happen next as they pushed me down the hall.

My mother-in-law and a nurse helped me out of my wet pajamas and into a hospital gown. Before I could get in the bed, there was a doctor in the room and another nurse. While the nurse prepped the skin on the back of my hand for an IV, I closed my eyes tight and hoped that it wouldn't hurt. After feeling a burning sensation, I looked down at my hand, and the IV had been inserted properly.

The nurse then wrapped a device around my stomach that monitored the baby's heart rate and measured my contractions. She explained everything as she asked me about how much pain I was in. As I told her the pain was pretty intense, I had a contraction from out of this world. It felt like I was about to die again, and I then told the nurse that I wanted the strongest medicine they could give me. When Trent's mother left the room, the doctor checked me, and I had dilated three centimeters. "Alright Mrs. Morrison all you have to do is dilate seven more centimeters, and your baby will be here," said the doctor, as he took his gloves off and dropped them in the trash bin.

After the doctor left, Trent entered the room and stood at the head of my hospital bed. "I called your mom. She's on the way. She also said that she would call your dad and let him know that you're having the baby."

"Alright," I said breathlessly, as I cringed in pain and shouted, "I need something for pain, and I need it now. I can't take this."

The nurse notified the doctor that I wanted something for pain, and he returned quickly. After being in so much pain and discussing my options, I decided to get an epidural and felt better immediately. Within the next thirty minutes, Mom and Ron showed up. When I saw her face, I felt like I was a baby all over again.

As she leaned in to give me a hug, I wrapped my arm that had the IV stuck in it around her as far as I could reach. I didn't want to let her go; I wanted to squeeze her. Her arms were so comforting that I almost forgot I was going to give birth soon. After we talked a little, I felt drowsy and slipped off into a light sleep. I could hear everyone talking, but I didn't respond to anyone. While I lay there with my eyes closed I wondered what was going to happen next; then my mind wandered to Melody.

I don't think anyone noticed the tears that slid out of the corners of my shut eyes. While I lay on my side, the tears fell onto my pillow, and I felt more emotional now than ever. I wasn't sure if it was the medicine from the epidural or if I truly felt this way. Whatever the reason, I wished that Melody were here with me now. I would do anything if she could be here to hold my hand or just sit at the foot of my hospital bed.

I didn't know how long I was asleep, but I woke up when I felt a lot of pressure on my bladder. The room was dim, but I noticed that Trent and Mom were the only two people in the room. It was a little after two in the morning, according to the digital clock on the wall, and I was very thirsty.

"I'm thirsty, my mouth feels like the Tin Man's did on *The Wizard of Oz*," I said in a dry voice.

Mom laughed and then replied, "You've been having some big contractions, I'm surprised you slept through them."

"I'll see if they have something for you to drink at the nurses' station," Trent said, as he slipped out the door.

"You'll probably deliver soon," Mom announced as she came and stood by the bed.

As soon as she put her hand on the side of my stomach, I felt a sharp pain. When Trent returned, he held a Styrofoam cup filled with small ice cubes.

"The nurse said that you could only have these," he said, as he dipped a plastic spoon into the cup and put a few tiny ice cubes on it.

While everyone talked, I fell in and out of sleep until the nurse woke me up and told me that it was time to check my cervix again. As the doctor felt around my private area, I felt a lot of pressure and got the urge to push. "It's time to start pushing Lyric; you've dilated ten centimeters," the doctor said while the nurses folded the lower half of the hospital bed down.

The pressure grew more intense, and the doctor told me to spread my legs wide, I definitely knew how to do that. But this time, I knew it would be a lot of pain and no pleasure involved. While mom stood on one side of the bed and Trent stood on the other side of the bed, I pushed without the doctor telling me too. "I see the baby's head," the doctor said while the nurse adjusted the mirror on top of the bed. I didn't like the feeling that I felt, but I pushed again just as the doctor told me to. "Good job. Now take a few deep breaths and push again," he said.

The very next push, I gave it my all and I delivered my baby. She was all slimy and gross looking until they cleaned her up. She cried as they wrapped her in a blanket and handed her to me. Trent was in awe, and my mom was crying. When I looked down, I saw that she looked exactly like me when I was a baby. I was in love; I had a little slice of Melody right here in my arms.

"Hello Brooklyn," I said, and her eyes fluttered.

That was the very first time I saw her eyes. They were the same color as Jason's and my fathers. A lump formed in my throat, and I couldn't say anything.

"Her eyes are beautiful," Trent said.

Mom then added, "She gets those beauties from her Papa, Rico Russo."

I'd been in so much guilt that I almost missed the perfect opportunity to chime in, "Yes, those are definitely Dad's eyes," I said as mom took the baby from me and handed her to Trent.

After we all held Brooklyn, they took her to the nursery. I was so glad that was over, and I hoped that someone would give me something to drink now. The nurse brought me a chilled can of ginger-ale, and I drank it all in one big gulp it seemed. After I was all cleaned up, I was moved to another room. This room was smaller, but it was just as nice as the delivery room. By this time Mom had gone home and I made calls to my father, Raven, and Latria.

Dad was working in Puerto Rico and suggested that we video chat as soon as we got settled in with Brooklyn at home. Before he got off of the phone, he said, "I hear that my granddaughter has my blue- gray eyes." My stomach felt a little queasy as I replied, "Yes daddy, she does." My older sister Raven planned to visit soon, and Latria said that she was coming to the hospital tomorrow after she got off work.

I was happy to talk to all of them, but I was beyond exhausted and fell asleep on Tent as we talked about how perfect Brooklyn was. The last thing I remembered was him asking me if I was going to breastfeed. That night I slept like a queen in her castle until the room door opened and woke me up. When the light from the hallway flooded in, I saw the nurse that had been in the delivery room with me. "I'm sorry to bother you, but I was coming to see if you wanted to try to breastfeed. My shift is almost over, and the baby is awake. After being with you through your labor and birth of your beautiful baby girl, I wanted to show you a few ways to hold her while she's nursing."

After looking at the clock and back at the nurse, I said, "Sure, I'm awake now."

"Great, I'll be right back, I'm going to get the baby."

"Alright," I replied, as I felt one of my breasts. It was gigantic and looked as though I'd had a boob job. I took both of my hands and felt myself up. These boobs were perfect, but they were sore. "Ouch," I said, out loud as I squeezed one of my nipples.

"What's wrong?" Trent said as he turned over on the tiny roll away bed.

"My boobs are hard as rocks, and one of them is leaking," I replied as I looked down at the wet spot starting to form on my hospital gown.

Trent got up and felt my breasts in curiosity.

"Damn, they are hard," he agreed as he touched them.

He then jerked his hand away from my milk filled breast as the nurse knocked on the door and opened it.

"Here's your little angel. Are you ready?" The nurse said as she rolled the baby to my bedside.

"Yeah, I think so," I answered, as I unfastened the hospital gown and let my breasts fall out.

After the nurse put a pillow on my lap, she picked up the baby and complimented her eyes. She was so adorable that I stole a kiss from her as the nurse situated her fragile body on a pillow. After the nurse guided me through the mini breastfeeding seminar, I felt like a professional. Brooklyn started sucking like a little pig and drank until her eyes fluttered to a close. Next, the nurse showed me how to burp her, and I softly patted her on her back until a small burp came out. "That was simple," I said as the nurse took Brooklyn and placed her back into the baby cart. "You did a great job. Most women have trouble with breastfeeding. I'm proud of you."

Trent sat in silence as the nurse, and I talked for a few more minutes before she announced that she had to clock out.

"Would you like Brooklyn to stay here with you or would you like for me to take her back to the nursery?"

"Umm, you can leave her here. I want to watch her sleep," I confessed.

"Alright, I'll see you tonight. Keep up the good work," the nurse said as she left the room.

"That went well," Trent said.

"Yes, it did."

Just then my stomach growled, and Trent's phone rang. He quickly answered it and said, "Good morning Mom. Yeah, I'm going to come and get Tia. I know she can't wait to see the baby. Alright mom, I'll see you in a bit," he said. "Tia can't wait to see the baby. I'm going to go and get her. Did you want me to get you a bite to eat on the way back?" He asked as he walked into the bathroom.

"Sure, I want a steak biscuit with egg and cheese. Can you stop at Hardee's?"

"Yep, I should be back by 8:30. Mom should have Tia dressed and ready to go."

Before Trent left, he bent down and kissed Brooklyn on the cheek. She didn't flinch and continued to sleep.

"I love you; I'll be back in no time. Try to go back to sleep. As much as Brooklyn had eaten, she should be asleep for a while," Trent said.

"Yeah you're right. Turn the light off on your way out and I'll try to catch a nap."

After Trent turned off the light, he left the room. I thought about calling Jason, but I remembered what happened the last time I was in the hospital, when Trent overheard me on the phone with Mont. I didn't want that to happen again, so I turned over and went to sleep.

I'm not sure how long I was asleep before I heard the hospital room door open again. I thought it was Trent and Tia, so I turned around with a smile only to see Mont looking down at Brooklyn in the baby cart.

"Mont, what are you doing in here?" I asked as I sat up in the bed.

"Believe it or not, I was going to get my girl some coffee, and I saw your name on the outside of the door."

What? Why is your fiancée here? Does she work here or something?"

"No, Lyric. She gave birth early this morning. I'm a father now," he said with a smile.

"You're not pulling my leg are you, Mont?" I asked as I pulled the covers up over my swollen breasts.

"Nah, I would never do that," he said, as he added, "I saw your baby in the nursery early this morning when they took my baby back there. My mother actually pointed her out to me and said how pretty her eyes were. I didn't know that she belonged to you. Congratulations."

"Thank you. Congratulations to you too."

"Well, I'd better get going before this coffee gets cold. Maybe, I'll see you around sometimes," he said before he reached for the door lever.

"Mont, I'm sorry. I shouldn't have ignored you. I wanted to call you and respond to your text messages, but I was afraid that you were going to show up at my house again."

Without turning around, he said, "That's okay. I still love you. Just remember what I said. I'll always be here for you. If Trent steps out again, don't go to Stone Dale Court, come to my house."

Then he blew me a kiss and left. I was puzzled as to how he knew about me moving out and going back to mom's house. I wasn't surprised that he'd known. He probably knew about Jason and the rendezvous that we had for that week when he was here. That was one thing about Mont. He had his ways of finding out stuff.

Twenty minutes after Mont left the room, Trent and Tia walked in. Brooklyn was still asleep in the baby cart when Tia walked over and pressed her face up against the plastic container. "She's perfect Mommy Lyric," she said, as she tried to hop up on the hospital bed but kept sliding off. With Trent's help, Tia snuggled beside me and kicked her sandals off. While she wiggled her toes, I kissed her on the top of her head.

"I got your food, it should still be hot," Trent announced, as he handed me the paper bag stained with grease drippings.

"I can't wait to chow down on this," I said, as someone knocked on the room door.

My heart dropped all the way down to my toes as I took a deep breath. Before I could say anything, a female voice said, "Good morning, I have your breakfast Mrs. Morrison." She then brought a green tray of food in and set it on top of the rolling table.

"Good morning," I said as I sat the greasy food bag in between Tia and me.

"Is this the baby girl that everyone has been talking about with those beautiful eyes?" She asked as she took a step closer to the baby cart.

"I think so," I replied.

"She is a doll. Aww, look at her. Congratulations to the both of you," she said.

"Thank you," Trent and I replied in unison.

As she left the room, I looked at Brooklyn and saw that she was wide awake. I told Trent to slide the breakfast tray over to the bed and the baby cart. "Look Tia. Brooklyn is awake. I think that she's ready to meet her big sister." Tia's eyes grew bigger by the second as I reached into the baby cart and picked up Brooklyn. I held her tightly and asked Tia if she wanted to hold her. "Can I really hold baby Brooklyn?" She asked excitedly.

"Yep," I said as Trent got up and stood on the other side of Tia. While they entertained Brooklyn, I ate the biscuit and hash browns from the greasy bag and the fruit and coffee off of the tray. I was beyond full, and I was ready to take a shower when Brooklyn started to fret. Her face grew red, and she made a frowny face. I didn't know if she was hungry or if she had wet her diaper, so I stuck my finger on the inside and got a little surprise.

"Eww, that's nasty," Tia said. I almost gagged when I looked at the dark colored baby poop on my finger. "Yeah, that is nasty," I agreed, as Trent reached over and took Brooklyn. Before I got up, I made sure that my gown was closed in the back and stumbled into the bathroom with the IV pole to wash my hands. When I came out of the bathroom, Trent had already changed Brooklyn and had just tossed the poopy diaper into the trash bin. I was glad that I didn't have to change the diaper, but I did have to feed her, so I sat back on the bed and pulled one of my breasts out.

Tia looked at me like I was crazy and I quickly told her to look away as Trent handed Brooklyn to me. When she latched on, I told Tia that she could look again. As she watched Brooklyn enjoy her warm milk, she started to ask questions and I tried to explain breastfeeding to her. The look on her face told me that she was confused, but she said, "Okay Mommy Lyric." After Brooklyn got her belly full, I burped her and handed her to Trent. She fell asleep on his chest while I waited for the nurse to bring me a fresh hospital gown.

When the nurse knocked on the door of the hospital room, I got up and opened the door. She handed me the gown and told me to let her know if I needed anything else. When I was about to shut the door back, I noticed a fancy hot pink and silver sign that read, "It's a Girl." I didn't recall Trent mentioning anything about putting a door banner up. *"This had to be from Mont,"* I thought as I closed the room door and prepared to shower.

Two days later Brooklyn and I were released from the hospital. Trent drove a few miles under the speed limit on our way home, and we made it home safe. When we pulled into the yard, there were no cars there. I was expecting Trent's mother to be here at least. I had to admit, I was a little nervous. I was glad that Trent knew what to do with a baby. While I unpacked my things from the hospital, Trent and Tia took Brooklyn into her nursery. After I started a load of laundry, I joined them and sat in the rocking chair near the window.

I felt a bit exhausted as Trent mentioned dinner. I hope he didn't think I was going to cook. I just gave birth to an 8 pound baby four days ago. I could walk, but my legs still felt a little weak and I was bleeding like there was no tomorrow. All I wanted to do was pull the sheets back on my bed and go to sleep for ten straight hours. I didn't know what it was going to be like tonight without the nurses here helping. I only knew that I was going to sleep as soon as Brooklyn went back to sleep.

I ended up falling asleep in the rocking chair and woke up to a semi dark room. My breasts ached as I heard Brooklyn crying from down the hall. I quickly sprinted to my bedroom and saw her in the middle of our bed. Trent was asleep on one side of her, and Tia was sleeping on the other side. Just as I stepped closer to the bed, Tia woke up and called Trent's name. "Daddy Brooklyn is crying," she said. When he saw me standing there, he slid over and patted the mattress beside him. I lay down in between Trent and Brooklyn and pulled one of my breasts out. After I propped Brooklyn up on a pillow, I leaned against Trent and went back to sleep.

14

How Time Flies

Four months passed by in no time and life was hectic. It seemed that I never had a moment alone. I couldn't tell you the last time I'd been over to Latria's house or the last time I had a drink of alcohol. I was still breastfeeding Brooklyn, and she stuck to me like glue. She actually preferred Tia or me over Trent. I guess that was because she was home with the both of us all day. Brooklyn was spoiled rotten, and she even slept in our bed every night. I was beyond exhausted and tried to sleep when she slept. Sometimes I let Tia watch Brooklyn while I took a quick shower. Tia treated her like one of her doll babies; she was really a big help, and I was happy to have her around.

Brooklyn's looks had changed a lot since she was a newborn, but she still had those beautiful blue-gray eyes. Her skin was a few shades darker than mine, and her head was full of jumbo curls. I wondered what she would look like as she grew older. I truly didn't know if Brooklyn was Trent's or not, but he signed her birth certificate. So in the states eyes, he was the father. I sent Jason a picture of Brooklyn the same day that Trent went back to work, and he responded with a baby picture of him. I thought that Brooklyn looked just like me, but I was wrong. Brooklyn looked like Jason, without a doubt she belonged to him, but we were the only ones who knew the truth, and we were going to keep it that way.

I was sleeping good until I got kicked in the back. Trent had to do something about Brooklyn sleeping with us. The reason we had a nursery was for her to sleep in it. All the things that we'd gotten as gifts at the baby shower or bought ourselves were going to waste. As I lay there with an inch of the mattress and a corner of the blanket, I thought back to how my life was without a husband and children.

The main thing I missed from my past was my freedom. The freedom to do whatever I wanted with whoever I wanted. Since I had the baby, Tia didn't go over to her Grammy's much anymore. She never wanted to be separated from Brooklyn. Another thing that I really missed was sleeping. I didn't know the last time I had an uninterrupted eight hours of sleep. Hell, I can't even remember the last time I had an uninterrupted three hours of sleep. Don't get me wrong, I love Tia and my baby, but I honestly felt like I was about to go insane.

I know I'm dead wrong for thinking like this, but I started to call Know Betta to see if I could go on tour with him for a week or so. I felt like I was wilting away here inside the house. I'd lost all of my baby weight except for five pounds. I wanted to strut my stuff, but it was kind of hard to do with two kids hanging onto you. With Brooklyn constantly looking for a boob to suck, I often thought about stopping with the breastfeeding. I have a few bags of milk in the freezer, and I planned on pumping more, so I could start giving Brooklyn her milk in a bottle.

That night I woke up to Brooklyn crying on the baby monitor. I felt terrible because Trent was sound asleep and this was the first night that we left her to sleep in her crib alone. I didn't know how long she'd been crying, so I quickly got up and walked down the hallway into her room.

The nightlight led me safely to the side of her crib without stubbing my toe on anything. Brooklyn was laying on her back screaming as loud as she could. Her sweet little face was as red as a beet. I immediately picked her up and tried to soothe her, but she was beyond ill and continued to cry.

I noticed right away that she had wet through her diaper, and the back of her pajamas was soaked. "Aww, mommy's poor baby. I'm going to get you cleaned up," I whispered as I sat her on the changing table. She piped down as soon as the wet clothes were off. I started to wipe her off in the bathroom sink, but remembered that there were plenty of warm wipes nearby in the wipe warmer. I never even knew that a wipe warmer existed until the day of the baby shower, I don't know who invented it, but I was so glad that they did.

After my princess was wiped off, powdered, and in a dry pair of pajamas, I sat in the rocking chair and fed her until she fell back to sleep. I thought about taking her back to bed with me, but that would defeat the purpose of her sleeping in her nursery tonight. She couldn't continue to sleep with us because she slept so wild and we needed our privacy. Ever since she'd been sleeping with us, we would surround Brooklyn with pillows and have sex in my closet or either in our master bathroom.

I'd almost forgot that the sheets were wet in the crib and nearly placed her on the wet spot. I didn't want her to wake up, so I walked softly with her tucked in my left arm like a football. When I reached the linen closet, I got two towels out and covered the small wet spot in the crib. I then put a crib sheet over the towels and put her in the crib. It was hard work with one arm, but I was right-handed, so the task of tucking the sheet in between the rail and the mattress was no problem at all. I feared that Brooklyn was going to wake up as soon as I put her down but she didn't. She did start to wiggle a bit, but I patted her softly on her back until she drifted off.

I stood and watched her for a few minutes, and she didn't move, so I headed back to bed. Trent was still asleep and hadn't even turned over. Before I lay down, I quietly walked over to his side of the bed and unplugged the baby monitor. While I was bent down on the side of Trent's nightstand, I heard a buzzing noise. I wondered what it was and looked around the floor on his side of the bed. I didn't see anything, so I went back to my side of the bed and plugged the baby monitor up in the electrical socket behind my nightstand.

I figured that I better relieve my bladder while I was up and that's exactly what I did. On my way to the bathroom, I heard the buzzing noise again. *What in the hell was that?* I thought to myself, as I tiptoed back to Trent's side of the bed. When I bent down I saw a green light flashing from under the nightstand. I stuck my hand through the opening and grabbed at whatever it was. I was shocked to see that it was a cell phone. As I looked on top of the nightstand, I saw Trent's phone. While the phone vibrated in my hand, Trent woke up and tried to grab it. I quickly ran into the bathroom and locked Trent out.

"Lyric, please baby, I can explain." Trent shouted through the door. "Whose phone is this Trent? Is it yours?" I asked, as I flipped the cheap phone open. There was a lock on the phone. After I entered Anna's birthday 7787, the phone didn't unlock. I tried a few more codes and the phone still didn't unlock. Just as I started to throw the phone against the wall, it started vibrating in my hand. Someone was calling Trent.

Since I couldn't break the code on the secret phone, I answered it, but I didn't say anything. The voice on the other end started talking "Hey baby. Thank goodness you answered. I can't find my panties. I think they're in your car somewhere, I thought I'd put them in my purse, but they're not in there." Then she giggled. I'm not sure if hearing her giggle set me off, or if it was the statement she said before the giggle. "Diamond, you are one trashy bitch, but I'm sure you already know that. You'll get what's coming to you. Just wait and see," I yelled. The voice didn't respond back, but she didn't have to because I knew that it was her. I remembered how she sounded when Latria and I called her at the jewelry store that day.

I knew that the kids were asleep, so I tried to keep my cool. I didn't want either of them to see us fighting. I was so glad that I didn't bring Brooklyn back to bed with me. As I opened the bathroom door, I saw Trent standing there with a sad look on his face. Without saying a thing, I grabbed his car keys off the dresser.

"What are you doing Lyric?" He asked in a whisper before I left the bedroom.

I took his keys and made a beeline for his car. After I unlocked it, I got in and locked the doors. While he ran down the sidewalk in his pajamas, I looked for Diamond's missing panties. When I didn't find them under the front passenger seat, I crawled through to the back seat and dug my hand down into the cushion. After I pulled out a small bottle of flavored body gel, I dug deeper and finally found what I was looking for. I held a pair of red lace thongs up for Trent to see as he peered inside of the car window. He watched me from the outside as I had a fit in his backseat.

After gathering myself, Trent tried to coax me out of the car. I totally ignored him as the thought of delivering Diamond her fancy panties crossed my mind. I knew that was exactly what I wanted to do as I climbed back into the front seat. Before I started the car, I adjusted the mirrors and seat.

"Lyric, get out of the car," Trent yelled, as he ran around to the driver's side window.

"Trent get the hell out of my way before I run you over," I shouted as I backed the car up like a race car driver.

When I pulled out of the driveway, I took a quick look back and saw Trent running back into the house. I wondered what he was about to do. Even though I wanted to leave a trail of fire down the highway, I considered that I had only had on a nightshirt and was driving without a license. As much as it killed me, I drove the speed limit on the short drive to Diamond's house. When I pulled up in her driveway, a motion light came on. All of her lights were off, but I knew she was up, and I knew that Trent probably warned her that I was coming.

I got out of the car with the panties in my left hand and walked up the steps to the porch. I tried to open her screen door, but it was locked, so I banged on it. I knew that she had to hear it. When I noticed that there was a doorbell, I pushed it several times. From the inside of the house I heard, "Ding- dong, ding-dong, ding-dong," shortly after that the front door came ajar and I saw a silhouette of her face. "You need to leave before I call the cops," she shouted with wide eyes. "You need to open this damn screen door and get your panties," I yelled. I didn't think she was going to do it, but she did.

Diamond opened the screen door and snatched the panties out of my hand. As she tried to close the door back, I pushed it open and snatched her outside on the porch.

"Don't you know that you're involved with a married man, you slut bucket? Do you know how dangerous this could be?" I snarled.

"Look, Lyric. There's no need to call me names and threaten me. Trent and I go way back. We've been messing around before he married Anna," she said, as she looked around to see if any of her neighbors were outside.

"I'm not going to go back and forth with you about Trent. If he wanted you to be his wife, he would've asked you to marry him and not me," I said, as I rolled my eyes.

"That's true, but why do I need to marry him if he comes running to me whenever I call. He's at my house more than he's home," Diamond said, with an attitude.

I swear to God that this chick was asking for it. I already had my fist clenched and it was only a matter of time before I gave her a knuckle sandwich.

"You're not the only one he's messing around with, he has more women, so I hope you don't feel special."

"I know. There's Cara, Morgan, and Stephanie. We all get together sometimes and things get pretty wild. I wished he would have invited you to one of our parties. I could have shown you a good time too," she said, as she looked down at my shapely legs in my short thin nightshirt. Then she said,

"You can come inside if you like, I would love to show you a few of my toys."

"You've got to be kidding me. If I go inside of your house I guarantee that you won't like what I do to you, so I'm going back home. Do yourself a favor and take my advice. Stay away from my husband," I screamed, as I walked back to Trent's car.

"Shake it, don't break it," Diamond said, as she whistled and checked me out on my way back to the car.

On the way back home, I had to call Latria. She most definitely had to hear about this right now. As soon as she answered, I spilled the beans. I told her everything. She sat in silence until I was done. "I think you should have gone inside," Latria said. "Are you serious, if I had gone inside I would have killed her crazy ass?"

"Well, what are you going to do?"

"I'm going to fight Trent when I get back home."

"Lyric, are you serious? Trent is way bigger and stronger than you. Are you sure you want to do that?"

"Umm, yep! I'm sure," I said, as I pulled up my driveway and got out of the car. "I've got to go, I'm home now if you don't hear anything from me in an hour call the police," I said as I hung up.

Trent was standing in the doorway when I walked onto the front porch. He opened the door for me, and I walked by him like he was invisible.

"Come on Lyric. Aren't you going to talk to me?" He asked.

My original plan was to ignore him, but he continued to pester me until it happened. I hit Trent upside the head with the baby monitor. As he held the back of his head, I told him exactly how I felt. "Don't you understand, I don't want to talk to you, and I don't want to hear anything that you've got to say? I've had it up to my eyeballs with you and your lies. What the hell is wrong with you? Do you have some type of sex problem or something? Diamond told me about the type of games you guys like to play. She also told me about Cara and.." Before I could finish my rant, Trent made a confession.

"Lyric, I do have a problem. I should've told you before we got married, but I was afraid that you wouldn't marry me if you knew that I was addicted to sex. I'm a nymphomaniac, and I have frequent sexual urges throughout the day that have to be fulfilled. That's why I always go to Diamond's house. She satisfies all of my sexual fantasies. She introduced me to threesomes and a lot more crazy stuff that you probably don't want to hear about. I'm sorry about this entire thing. I really love you, but I can't promise you that I can remain faithful to you."

"What do you mean remain faithful to me? You've been cheating on me since the day we got back from our honeymoon. I can't believe this shit. How could you be so selfish? Did you even think about Tia's feelings getting hurt while you were out having threesomes and partaking in orgies? You're not the man I thought you were, and I'm sorry that I ever got involved with you," I hissed.

"Lyric don't say that, if you never got involved with me we wouldn't have Brooklyn, and of course, I thought of Tia's feelings, but I just can't seem to control myself. Maybe I should try counseling again. I was going to counseling sessions twice a week before Anna died. We were actually in the process of getting a separation the month before she had Tia. I'm so ashamed of myself. This disorder is ruining my life," he said, as he sat on the side of the bed and covered his face with his hands.

Trent was right. If I hadn't married him, we wouldn't have Brooklyn because I wouldn't have met Jason in Hawaii. I guess I was glad that I'd met Trent because without him, I wouldn't have my baby girl. So something good did come out of this sham of a marriage, but I was still curious to know how he'd met Diamond.

"I hope I don't regret asking you this, but how did you meet Diamond?" I inquired, as I sat down beside him.

"I met her at the jewelry store; this was before she owned her store. I was shopping for an engagement ring for Anna, and she pointed me in the right direction. I looked through a catalog in the store for hours trying to find Anna the perfect ring. When I couldn't make my mind up, Diamond helped me customize Anna's engagement and wedding ring. After the ring order had been completed, she gave me her business card. A few days later I went to a bar and ran into her and a few of her friends. That same evening she invited me to her house, and I accepted the invitation. Ever since then, I've been hooked on the way she does things. I've never met a woman that can do the things that she does," he confessed.

"Damn, I should've gone inside, she probably could have taught me something," I thought before I asked Trent another question.

"Why didn't you marry her then if she's so wonderful and great?" I asked sarcastically.

"That's a simple question. I didn't marry her because I don't love her. I only love how she makes me feel."

"Oh, well. I guess that makes sense," I said.

"So, what are we going to do?" He asked.

"Do you think that counseling could work for you?" I asked curiously.

"I'm not sure, but it's worth a try. I don't want to lose you."

I felt bad for Trent, so I reached up and rubbed the back of his head. A small knot had already surfaced where the baby monitor made contact with his noggin.

That night Trent slept out on the couch, and I had the bedroom to myself. Even though I wasn't extremely mad at him anymore, I didn't want to sleep with him. After I rinsed the bits of dirt and grass off of my feet, I called Latria and told her everything that Trent said word for word. She couldn't believe it and planned on coming by tomorrow after she got off work. Before she hung up, she asked, "Do you really think that counseling is going to change him?"

"I'm not sure, I'll keep my fingers crossed" I replied.

"I'll keep my fingers crossed too, but just in case this doesn't work, make sure you have a backup plan," she said.

"When you say backup plan, do you mean Mont?" I asked.

"Duh, get off of the phone with me and call him. He said that he would be waiting. Remember?" Latria replied as she laughed and hung up.

As soon as Latria and I were off of the phone, I called Mont. His phone rang three times before he answered.

"Hey, are you busy?" I asked.

"Nah, not at all. How are you? I've been thinking about you," he said.

"I'm okay; I've been thinking about you too."

"You don't sound like you're okay. Did something happen?"

"Yeah, something did happen, but I think I'll be alright," I assured Mont as I let out a deep breath.

"Why are you holding back? I know you well enough to know when something is going on with you. Stop bullshitting around and tell me what happened before I come over there," He barked.

"Mont, please don't. Tonight has been crazy enough. If you really want to know what happened, I'll tell you." I blurted.

Ten minutes later Mont knew everything that happened between me, Trent, and Diamond. All he had to say was, "If you keep allowing this dude to disrespect you like that, he's going to keep playing you. You don't deserve this Lyric. You need me in your life. I've changed, being a daddy to a little girl has opened my eyes. I'm ready to treat you like I'd want someone to treat her."

"You're right, I do deserve better. I'm glad that you were able to talk to me tonight. I'm thankful for your friendship," I confided.

"So you're just going to keep me in the friend zone?" He asked with a chuckle.

"Mont, I'm still married, and you have a live-in girlfriend or fiancée or whatever you want to call her, did you forget about them that fast?"

"My girl and I broke up a month or so before she gave birth. Believe it or not, I caught her cheating and gave her the boot. She moved in with her aunt, she doesn't live too far away, so I get to see my princess, at least four times a week," he answered.

"Oh well, I tell you what. If the counseling doesn't work out, we can give it another shot. I can't lie, I miss you like crazy."

"I'd like that. This time around is going to be different. I just hope that I get a chance to show you," he said.

As much as I hated to end the call with Mont I had to because I heard Brooklyn crying on the baby monitor. I couldn't believe that it still worked after I hit Trent upside the head with it. "Mont, I've got to go Brooklyn is crying. Maybe, I'll call you tomorrow. I love you" I said. "I sure hope so, and I love you too," he replied. I could tell that he was smiling through the phone. He was on cloud nine, and I was too. After talking to him, I secretly hoped that counseling didn't work for Trent. As a matter of fact, I couldn't wait for him to mess up again.

15

Third Times a Charm

After a month of trying to make things work with Trent, I threw in the towel. Our marriage hadn't survived a year, and a half and it was officially over. I'd had enough of Trent, his lies, and his disorder. I planned on filing for a legal separation as soon as I could after I drove by Diamond's house and saw his car parked in the driveway. The last thing I wanted to do was make a scene considering that the girls were with me. They were buckled safely in their car seats while my blood came to a boil in the front seat. Tia wasn't aware of anything; she watched a movie on her portable DVD player while sleepy head Brooklyn slept peacefully.

A part of me wanted to drive the car straight into the house. But I knew that one of the kids would get hurt if I did that, so I calmly pulled over on the side of the street and put the car in park. I was going to call Trent, but didn't, I knew that would lead to yelling and shouting, and I didn't want to get the kids upset. I only snapped a picture of his car in Diamond's driveway and sent it to him along with a text message that read, "It's over." I waited for a few moments, but Trent didn't respond. I guess he and Diamond were getting busy or something because he didn't message me until two hours later. By that time, I had already gone to a lawyer's office and got some advice about the separation process in the state of Virginia.

I had a better understanding of what I needed to do after I talked to the lawyer. After me and the kids left the lawyer's office, my stomach growled, and I decided to go home and cook. With the girls settled in the living room in front of the television, I prepared dinner. When our meal was almost ready, Trent finally called.

"I can explain" he assured as I answered.

"Explain? There's absolutely no need to explain. I saw your car over there Trent. You're busted" I cursed.

"Lyric, don't be like that. I'm on my way home. I'm sure we can work this out."

"Home? What home? You don't have a home anymore. If you come here, Brooklyn and I are leaving. We'll go to Stone Dale Court," I threatened.

"You can't break up the girls. Not tonight. That's not right," he stuttered.

"Oh yes, I can. Apparently, you don't give a damn about me or the girls. It's not me breaking up the family; it's you. You can't seem to stay away from Diamond," I hissed.

"Yes I can," he spat out.

"Well, Trent, I'm not going to give you any more chances. I'm disgusted with your behavior, and clearly the counseling isn't working. You made your bed. Now you're going to have to lie in it," I said, as I ended the call.

After I hung up, I turned on the computer and printed all the evidence that I'd collected during our marriage. I made sure not to print out the pictures of Jason I'd collected, as I gathered the papers in a neat pile and put them on top of the refrigerator out of Tia's reach. Not even ten minutes later Trent walked through the door. Tia greeted him with her usual hug, and Brooklyn jabbered at him as he picked her up out of her high chair. "What's for dinner?" He asked as he bent down and kissed me on my cheek.

"Oh no, he didn't!" I thought to myself. Trent was so close to getting his lips ripped off that it wasn't even funny. I tried to hide my ill feelings for him while we were in front of the girls, but I couldn't keep my composure much longer. That's when I asked if I could talk to him in the bedroom. As he walked towards our room, he carried Brooklyn in his arms. "Leave Brooklyn in here with Tia," I boldly said as I reached to grab the stack of papers from the top of the refrigerator.

"I'm ready to eat. Can you make this quick?" He said as he walked into the room and closed the door.

"I'm sorry. Did you bump your head while you were at Diamond's house? You're not eating here tonight, and you're damn sure not sleeping here tonight either," I snapped as I threw the printed evidence in his direction.

"What in the hell is all those papers?" He asked.

"Oh, that's proof of your dirty dog ways. You can't deny this. You know these nude pictures came from your phone. Don't play dumb."

"Really Lyric, you're going to kick me out?"

"Yes. I told you, either you leave, or Brooklyn and I leave. That's it."

"Why you got to make this so hard? Can you give me one more chance?"

"Hell no! You need to pack your things and get the hell out, or I'll start packing it for you."

After accepting the ultimatum, Trent packed as much of his stuff as he could into three suitcases and two big black trash bags. Before he left, he asked Tia if she wanted to go with him or stay with Brooklyn and me. She chose to stay with us, and I wasn't surprised. I knew that she loved me as much as her dad, but she really wanted to be with Brooklyn. After

Trent gathered the rest of his things, he kissed the girls good night and left. I then locked the front door and set the alarm.

With Brooklyn in her playpen and Tia entertaining her with a pile of teddy bears in the living room, I realized that I needed a moment alone. My eyes watered as I made my way to my bedroom. Clothes were scattered everywhere, and a few drawers were left open on the dresser. I watched my step as I walked through a trail of wire hangers that Trent had left on the floor. I felt so emotional standing in the middle of this mess; this did not seem real. Now that my husband was gone, how would I pay the bills? The house payment alone was over $1,000 a month, and I hadn't worked in a year. I had $4,000 in my savings account, and a little more than $6,500 in the safe in mom's closet.

I hadn't worked since I had gotten fired from the Dentist office and I didn't have any sugar daddies depositing money into my bank account. My cash flow had been at a standstill for a while now; I couldn't believe that I was in this predicament. I guess if I had to, I could ask Dana for some money and keep my fingers crossed that she wouldn't want anything in return. Or, I could call Know Betta and ask for a loan, I knew he had it.

As soon as I thought about Know Betta, I remembered the talk I had with him about moochers. If I called him and asked him for money- would I be considered a moocher? *"Gosh, I hate this,"* I thought to myself as I wet a washcloth and wiped my tear stained face. After I was done sulking, I folded the washcloth in half and placed it on the counter. My bangles jingled as I walked out of the bathroom. When I looked down at them, they sparkled and shined. I knew that these things had to be worth a pretty penny and decided that if worse came to worst, I would pawn my bangles before I had to ask Dana or Know Betta for anything.

That very next day the lawyer drew up the separation papers and Trent agreed to sign them. I felt free as soon as he scribbled his signature on the forms. I still had his last name, but I knew that it was only a matter of time before we would be able to get a divorce. With all the evidence that I had, his lawyer suggested that he give me the house and pay child support for Brooklyn. Trent and I both decided that Tia would stay with Brooklyn and me on the weekends and that she would stay with him at his mom's house on the weekdays. I hated that it had to be this way, but in actuality Tia wasn't my child, so Trent had the final say-so about her staying. I loved her just as much as I loved Brooklyn and I hated that Trent ruined not only our marriage, but hurt Tia in the process.

The first weekend he dropped her off, she was so happy to see me, and she held Brooklyn for hours, even though she squirmed and tried to get away. I was still ill with Trent and stopped him at the front door when he dropped Tia off. I didn't want to see his no good face. I couldn't believe that he played me like that. Now that we were separated, I talked to Mont every day and even reached out to Jason and told him everything that had been going on. When he offered me an invitation to bring Brooklyn to Hawaii, I didn't hesitate to accept his offer because I needed a vacation more than ever.

We flew out on a Monday and stayed in a fancy hotel near the red restaurant where Jason worked. He welcomed Brooklyn and me with beautiful leis. My lei had yellow, orange, and pink flowers. Brooklyn's lei was different shades of pink; she looked absolutely adorable wearing it. As soon as he saw her, he confessed his love for her and admitted that he was infatuated. Brooklyn seemed to like Jason and even cried for him when he had to leave us to go to work. She must've known that he was her father. She never cried for Trent like that.

We only went to the ocean and the pool at the hotel while we were there. It was great spending time in Hawaii with Jason; he was a complete gentleman. While Jason took Brooklyn to the kiddie pool, I people watched and saw a few hunks that Latria might be interested in. I laughed to myself as I thought of what she might say to the good looking guys on the beach. Maybe I could bring Latria to Hawaii the next time I came. She had to see these men for herself. The pictures that I snapped of them when they weren't looking weren't good enough. I knew that she would want to see them live and in living color.

The night before we left Jason cooked dinner for me. He stole kisses from Brooklyn as she watched him cook on the stovetop. He turned me on and I hoped that he made a move on me tonight I hadn't had sex for a while, and I really wanted him. We only kissed a few times since we'd been here and I was thirsty for more.

We ate our grilled steak, vegetables, and mashed potatoes on the balcony. We couldn't see the beach, but we could hear the waves crashing against the shore, and that was good enough for me. I was relaxed, and the glass of wine I drank had gone straight to my love box. As my temperature started to rise, I remembered the sex Jason and I had back in Virginia.

Just then Brooklyn started nodding, and her face almost fell into a pile of mashed potatoes. Jason and I laughed as he cleared the small table and took the dishes inside. "I'm going to give Brooklyn a bath before she goes to sleep," I said, as I headed towards the bathroom with her. "Brooklyn you're a party pooper," he said, as he followed me. After Jason helped with Brooklyn's bath, I gave her a bottle and she went to sleep. Then Jason put her on the bed and joined me out on the balcony.

We both drank another glass of wine and enjoyed the warm night breeze. Without warning, I stood up and straddled his lap. The dress that I wore allowed him easy access to my love box. We kissed until I was dizzy. My breathing changed as he caressed my behind and slid my thong to the side. After he fumbled with his zipper, I came to my senses and asked him to put on a condom. I stood up for a second so he could remove his pants and retrieve the condom out of his wallet. After he slid the condom on, I eased down on his erection and began to grind on him. Jason's hips came to life and moved back and forth. He held me by my waist and pumped madly inside of my wetness. "Slow down, you don't want the condom to break again," I said. Jason slowed down, but only after he said, "We make beautiful babies together, we should make another one." I wondered if he was serious as his lips sucked at the tender skin of my neck. At that moment, I didn't care. I was in Hawaii in the arms of this gorgeous man, who put out the burning fire that was buried deep between my legs. Just as I thought Jason was finished, he surprised me by picking me up. He then turned me around and bent me over the rail on the balcony for a few more minutes of spine-tingling pleasure.

We had sex again in the shower before we lay down that night. I had a few hickeys on my neck, and I didn't mind at all because I didn't belong to anybody anymore. I put a few hickeys on Jason's neck too, and I gave him a blowjob that he wouldn't forget anytime soon before we called it a night. Brooklyn slept in between the both of us. When I woke up in the middle of the night, Jason had Brooklyn on top of his chest. They looked so precious that I had to snap a picture of them before I went back to sleep.

The next morning Jason had to go to work, so he woke me up before he was about to leave.

"I'm about to go, my sweet. Last night was wonderful by the way," he said, as he kissed me.

"Yes, it was. I really enjoyed myself this week," I replied, as I wrapped my arms around him.

"Let me know when you're ready to come back for a visit. I'd love to see Brooklyn again."

"I'll do that," I responded.

"Tell Brooklyn that Daddy loves her when she wakes up," he said, as he bent down to kiss her on the cheek.

As soon as Jason left I received a text message from him that read, "I miss her already." I quickly sent him the picture I'd taken of the two of them last night. He responded with a smiley face and asked me to send him a text message when we made it to the airport. I did as he asked, as soon as Brooklyn and I made it through the security check. The plane ride was long, and we slept most of the way. When we touched down in Virginia, I sent Jason a text message to let him know that we'd made it home safe. That same night Trent came over and asked if he could take Brooklyn to the movies with Tia. At first, I was going to tell him no, but I needed some alone time, so I let him take her.

I slept like it was nobody's business. When I woke up, I had missed calls from Mont and Jason. I called Jason first. He only asked about the flight and wanted to know if I could set up a video chat with him and Brooklyn sometime this week. After I got off of the phone with him, I called Mont back. I knew that he wanted to see me, but I let him beat around the bush and eventually asked him if he wanted to come over. I hopped in the shower before he came and put on a pair of pajamas. Just as I put my hair in a ponytail, I heard the doorbell ring. It was Mont and he came with a vase of flowers. As I sat the beautiful bouquet on the coffee table, I wondered if he used the same florist I got Melody's flowers from. After I thanked him for the flowers, I gave him a hug and we got comfortable on the sofa. While we watched a movie on *Showtime* we talked over a bowl of potato chips. Believe it or not, Mont and I didn't have sex that night. Before he left we did cuddle on the couch and exchange a few kisses, but that was it.

Five minutes after Mont left, Trent pulled in and dropped off Tia and Brooklyn. My hands were full, but that was okay because I had a nap. As the girls settled down, I focused my attention on finding a job. My mind led me to call the manager at the spa that I used to work at, and she welcomed me back with open arms. I was so excited that I had almost forgot about finding a daycare for Brooklyn to attend. After pricing a few places on the internet, I realized how expensive daycare was. Four hundred bucks a month was a bit much, so I called Trent's mom and asked her if she could keep Brooklyn for me during the week and she agreed. When I tried to discuss her pay, she stated that she wouldn't accept any money from me. "Brooklyn is my grandchild; we have the same blood flowing through our veins. You don't have to pay me one red cent," those were her exact words. *"If she only knew,"* I thought to myself.

A few months later I'd gotten into the swing of things and received my first paycheck. I was exhausted, but I didn't mind working hard to make ends meet. When I received the first child support check, I thought someone was playing a trick on me. I never imagined that I would get six hundred dollars a month for Brooklyn, I wasn't complaining at all though because I needed the money. Sometimes I thought about Trent, but it wasn't because I missed him. I thought about how he seemed different from all the other men I'd dated in the past, but he was worse. You really don't know what you're getting into when you meet a new person. I'm thankful that I met Trent because without him I wouldn't have Brooklyn. I couldn't imagine my life without her now. Since I'd kicked Trent to the curve, I kept my promise and gave Mont another chance.

That same weekend Trent decided to keep both Brooklyn and Tia. I thought I was going to be home alone until Mont called and asked me if he could come over. When I told him that the girls were staying with Trent, he insisted that I stay the night with him. I agreed to and quickly packed an overnight bag before I set the security alarm and drove across town to his house.

As I walked through the door, he ushered me into his bedroom and closed the blinds.

"Take off all of your clothes and get in bed," he instructed as he went back downstairs.

I wondered what Mont had up his sleeve when he came back with a can of whip cream, Jell-O cubes, and fruit roll ups. After he sat the tray of goodies down on the bed, he got undressed and climbed on top of me.

"Tell me that you'll be my wife one day," he said, as he looked into my eyes.

"Is that really what you want to hear Mont?"

"Yes, more than anything," he replied.

"Yes, I will be your wife one day," I confirmed, as I wet his lips with my tongue.

That evening, Mont and I had the freakiest, nastiest sex that you could ever imagine. He'd learned some new things, and I showed him a thing or two as well. Shortly after we were done, we showered and changed the sheets on the bed because they were wet with sweat and sticky from the edibles that he brought to bed with us. With the fresh sheets on the bed and the television on Mont and I chatted, and he gave me a set of keys to his house before he fell asleep.

I, on the other hand, lay there thinking. I had to admit it, it felt good to be with someone who truly loved me. I felt that deep down in my heart Mont had changed. Not only did we have our beautiful daughters that shared the same birthday, but we also had each other. I couldn't see my life getting any better than this. In the end, I not only had my house on the hill, but had a set of keys to Mont's mini mansion too.

After laying wrapped in Mont's arms for thirty minutes or so, I inched away from him. My bangles jingled, and I moved from the warmth of his body and sat up on the side of his bed. After I checked my phone, I saw that Latria had sent a text message that read, "I just heard that Trent got a promotion at work and started dating Diamond." "My feelings aren't hurt at all. I hope that he does her like he did me. Maybe she would learn her lesson when another beauty catches his eye. Then Diamond will get a dose of her own nasty medicine," I replied, as I powered the phone off and headed to the bathroom.

I didn't have to urinate; I just wanted to look at myself. The only thing I had on were my bangles. They jingled as I wrapped my loose hair up into a bun with a hair tie that was on the counter. I had to admit, I looked different, and I felt a bit worn out. I didn't have the same body that I had when I was a teenager. I had a few stretch marks and a little bulge in my tummy from where Brooklyn once resided.

As I stood there, I wondered how my life would be with Mont. *"Would I ever have my happily ever after? How would I deal with the mother of Mont's child? Should I take my bangles off again, but for good this time?"* That was the last thought that crossed my mind as I stood there. *"Maybe I should,"* I said to myself as I started taking them off one by one.

The shiny bands of gold clinked on the marble counter as I set each one down, then I quickly changed my mind and put them back on. At that moment, I realized that the bangles were never the problem. I was the problem and taking them off wouldn't change me. I would still be Lyric; I would still be attracted to men and maybe even a few women. *"The bangles were definitely staying,"* I thought to myself as I winked my eye at my reflection, turned the light off in the bathroom, and climbed back in bed with Mont.

CPSIA information can be obtained at www.ICGtesting.com
Printed in the USA
BVOW06s0301131016

464929BV00011B/40/P